Fleshworld

Carole Morin

龙
Dragon Ink
London

First published in the UK 2022 by Dragon Ink Ltd,
London.

A CIP catalogue record for this book is available from the British Library.

ISBN 978-0-9572089-5-7

Typeset by Dink, London.

Printed in the UK by
Imprint Digital, Devon EX5 5HY.

For Harry,

who always helped

Acknowledgements

Thanks to:
Society of Authors, Bad Fan,
Tony Bains, Andrew Catlin,
John Calder, Nick Cave,
Lee Carter, Jackie McGlone
and especially to Don Watson,
who makes everything possible.

'To face Heaven, you have to turn your back on Hell.'

Don Watson

Part One

Rich's Story

'Time heals everything except wounds.'
Chris Marker

I have always longed to be safe.

Even after inventing the vaccine, I didn't feel safe. Was I programmed to expect the worst? On the surface, her cruelty made me strong. But inside I am broken. I have lost my soul.

I know that something irreparable will happen. Something that I can't fix. It's only a matter of time. Injecting myself with Safe every morning can't protect me.

The crone cut me, leaving her mark. That wasn't it. It's something else. Something worse. Waiting for me in the black hole separating Pure World from Fleshworld; fulfilling her prophesy of doom.

Every day I think about it. Knowing it will come for me. Knowing it will get me. Impossible to escape.

Suddenly I stopped thinking about catastrophe. Stopped seeing the scissors attacking my secret part. That's not true. It wasn't sudden.

After marrying Ice, I thought about her. And before I married her, I obsessed about how I could have her. I was distracted. Perfecting my product, becoming even richer, protecting my beautiful Ice, keeping her safe. Even my sex scar stopped throbbing.

Ice changed everything. She never betrayed her perfection. She played her part; until she disappeared.

My fear has been hidden for so long I imagined it no longer existed. Hiding inside me with memories of Mother; the cackle creeping out of her that night she marked me.

Now all my scabs are on display. Fear consumes me. Covers my flesh with its vapour, preparing to expose me.

Fear I will never find my wife. Fear I will find her too late. She will no longer be my perfect Ice.

What if it's already too late? She is...infected.

And the dread, living inside me, odourless and sinister as the mist coming off the lake circling our bubble. She will discover my secret. She will find out what I have done. She will know what I am. Recoil from me in disgust. She will hate me, hate me, hate me.

Why didn't I take Ice to my island? We could be in Utopia now, drinking Martinis, safe in the blue glow of sea and stars; away from people and evil. Why did I do nothing except wait for fate to strike?

Now it is too late. Ice is gone. Lost. My nightmare is real. There is no end to my quest. Yet I cannot stop beginning.

The Beginning

It is easy to relate the story of her disappearance and imagine, convinced, that it is the start of everything.

But I know somewhere in my consciousness, deep in a place I prefer not to recognise, that the orgy is where it began. The flesh party she did not want to go to.

'How absurd,' she said, shaking back her glistening hair, a character in a fantasy already with her cigarette holder and eyes that never look swollen, even when she cries in the dark. 'We live in Pure World,' she went on, emphasising her point.

Orgies are not us. We are clean people.

At least I thought that was her point. Perhaps she was disdainful of depravity on this side of the border, when Fleshworld has a stranglehold on it? Chairman Luck owns the copyright on sex and its siblings: compulsion and lust.

That is one of the things I liked about her. You could never be sure what she was thinking.

We went to the flesh party. And I witnessed her

savage pleasure.

My heartbeat was speeding when we arrived at the safe house, a former royal palace, symbolic of the fetishisation of the past prevalent in our new world. I was scared the security system would pick up my anxious pulse, refuse me admittance.

There's a rumour the Chairman sometimes attends these parties. Participants are severely vetted. Only the super safe are admitted. Wealthy ancients inoculated against sex decay, the germ-free risk-takers defy the laws of Pure World; their exposed flesh revolting the eye.

'Let's go home,' I whispered into my wife's pale hair.

She moved through the door like she had not heard me. I wanted to grab her, pull her back. She's inside already, accepting a glass of love juice.

I love her. I love my wife. Why did I bring her here?

A sucker paused at her work to stare up at me. My eyes were drawn to a surprisingly long tongue that made me think of Mother.

By the time I averted my gaze, Ice was several rooms ahead of me. As I pursued her through inter-connected chambers, draped with damask and velvet, I made a business plan in my head. New bodies for the ancients. There's a fortune to be made in that. Not surgically altered. Their DNA inserted into a machine, creating a perfect new body attached to the lacquer masks that once were their faces.

It is my fault. I am the one who sold them *Safe*. A drug only ancients can afford to inject daily. Now they are taking turns fucking my wife.

Controlling my despair, I entered the flesh zone; an inner courtyard with a domed roof brilliant with mirror tiles.

Ice was consumed by the crowd. Her gleaming halo of hair reflected on the ceiling, then lost under a circle of panting admirers. The throng pushed me back until I could see nothing but exposed rears. But I know it is her being fucked. Who else would cause this excitement?

She didn't make a sound. Only vulgar women howl to indicate orgasm or despair. The flicker behind her blue eyelashes implied enjoyment. I have never noticed before. Does she always paint them blue?

She is not my wife anymore. She is a naked object. The focus of everyone's attention. Everyone wants to be her and fuck her.

I expected them to look. But did not imagine she would allow anyone to touch her.

Fury overwhelmed me as I shoved off the sucker kneeling before me, trying to push my way to the front. I must reach my wife.

Why did I bring her here?

An iron grip escorted me from the room, gliding me effortlessly to the door.

'Your presence is not desired.' A tall man, his expression somewhere between anger and shame, stood in front of a mirror observing my humiliation.

'This is a mistake...'

As the steel paw ejected me into the cold night air, I realised the tall guy is me.

I stood outside in the rain, imagining my wife being fucked.

Why did I make her come here?

She is doing this for me.

A lie, an excuse. It had been my idea to go, but she is the star of the show.

Had I wanted that? To show her off, show the other men what I owned, make them envy me? And then hated it when it happened. How can I blame her for that?

Beneath her perfect surface, is there thwarted passion she conceals from me? I have long suspected she has a secret. Everyone has secrets, why not her? It would be incredible if she did not have a secret admirer. A secret love?

When I got home Ice was in bed asleep already, tucked in safe under the clean white sheets, her left hand with its blue diamond dangling over the edge.

She does not look soiled. She is clean. *Safe.* I injected her myself before we went to the party. Her child's face is innocent in sleep. What is she dreaming about?

During the day her emotions are contained

within the mask of sophistication created in her dressing room. At night her secrets are concealed by the protection of sleep.

She loves me. I can tell from the way she looks at me when she wakes up to find me watching her. From the way she strokes my forehead, her cool fingers soothing the agitation in my head.

She cries out, her hand reaching for me in the dark. I hold her close, breathing in her perfume, happy.

I buried my fears. We didn't go to another flesh party. I banished the image of her pleasure. Surely I was mistaken?

Why did we stay here?

Every time I mentioned escaping to the island Ice said, *maybe*, or *later*, an impossible expression in her eyes as she sipped angel juice, staring at the sky. I did not know for sure then that she had her own secret. But I suspected.

The idea that Ice may leave me, was in love with another man, or not in love with me, was gnawing at me. And that old ingrown fear, implanted by Mother, the anxiety too banal to think out loud.

She married you for your money.

Of course she did. A beauty like Ice could never marry a poor man. Not now the city formerly known as London has split in two. Not now the world has turned toxic and everyone needs *Safe*.

The eternal lights of Fleshworld have erased the stars, but the moon is still there. The moon reminds me of the crone. Its grey glow looking down on us, out of reach but always watching, a whisper away from prophesy.

Greed distracted me. Fear that Ice would be stolen by somebody richer spurred me on. I must make more, increase my fortune, make sure there is enough. For what? To keep her safe. To protect her. To keep her forever.

We continued our perfect life. I made more money, becoming safer, making her love me more. She went for manicures and massages. There's more to her than that.

I can still feel her electric-blue nails scratching my flesh, making me bleed. Her toes clawing in the dark, scavenging under silk sheets for skin to break.

We were happy, safe in our glass bubble floating on the lake. Drinking dry Martini cocktails in the evening, changing the digital view from bright to stormy.

My wife loves old-fashioned drinks, reminders of an elegant world named the past. She loves rain. The sound soothes her as it washes the world. While inside our home everything is dry and clean. Nothing can touch us.

And then she disappeared.

The empty bubble disturbed me.

Not because I have never come home to find it empty before. But because I have. She's been missing a lot lately, coming home later and later. A familiar uneasy feeling filled me as I sniffed the air for her scent, knowing that I have misplaced my soul and will never recover it.

The word portentous annoys me. Mother had a tendency to use words she did not understand. But it describes the sensation in me as I entered Ice's empty bedroom. A feeling everything was about to change forever. I had lost control at last.

The room retains my wife's essence even when it is empty. In absence she can still be felt. I listened at her bathroom door, holding my breath. I'd hate to catch her in the act.

Her bathroom was a bomb site. Did she switch Slavia off so that she could sleep late? It was her idea to give the robot a name, like an old-fashioned servant. But she doesn't like Slavia touching her things. She doesn't like anyone touching.

Did she sleep late to avoid seeing me before I left for work? To avoid looking me in the eye before she's applied her mask. To wriggle out of kissing me goodbye?

Was she in a mad rush today? Maybe she forgot to switch Slavia back on because she was in a hurry to get somewhere? To meet someone...

The mess in her bathroom is evidence that she exists. It will keep me company until she gets home, the cheerful chaos revealing something about her.

I stared at her perfume. One bottle shattered on the floor, empty. One missing a lid. One upturned on the glass dressing table, but closed. Nothing dripping out of it. She has enough tinted bottles to open a perfume shop.

Trying to cover up her stink.

Mechanically, I turned the bottle upright, replaced the lid on the other, scenting her as I did this. I dislike catching sight of myself in the mirror. I do not need to be reminded.

The zip on the silver bag hidden behind the vanity mirror sounds too loud as I pull it open, like an alarm bell ringing somewhere in my future.

Hidden? It is not hidden. She has just put it there, absently. If she really wanted to hide something she wouldn't do it in here in full view of the camera.

'For your protection,' I told her, that first night, when she looked up and saw the light, trembling, in the fake sky of our roof.

Taking her lipstick out of the bag, a deep violet that brings out the blue in her skin, I resisted an impulse to write something on the mirror. I emptied out the contents of her silver purse, listening to them drop into the marble sink.

Eyeliner, lipstick, a small vial of something. Sniff it. Not perfume. Unless it has lost its scent, hidden in the dark too long.

Mr S Graham's card was tucked in a secret pocket in the lining of her purse. The same Mr S Graham? It must be. Though he was at a different location when I last consulted him. I never got confirmation of what the S stood for. Satan I presume.

Why does Ice have his card? Why would she need a lawyer? It doesn't cross my mind that they could be involved in something other than business together. Mr S Graham is not the type. He is not Ice's type. Does she have a type?

She's plotting to leave you.

Distracted by the sight of her underwear discarded in the bath. Not reduced to sniffing it yet. A snow bug was flicking around the light above her mirror. A pretty name to cover a lie. The sight of it astonished me. Almost beautiful, except its bite can kill.

Did it fly across the black hole from Fleshworld then refuse to die when confronted by the ice?

Reports of flesheaters escaping from the black hole, spreading their diseases around town, appear in the propaganda bulletin almost daily. I had assumed they were an invention intended to keep good citizens away from the border. To keep us safe.

But how did it get in? How did it get past Rob? He is programmed only to admit Ice and me. Is his scent detector failing? Can a plague of black death infiltrate our sanctuary?

Random thoughts surprised me.

The past is safe. The future a fantasy. The present is dangerous.

She's gone. Missing. Vanished.

Relief is supposed to follow long-anticipated dread. The nightmare is real and I'm staring at her knickers, thinking about a flesh-eating insect.

I flattened it against the mirror, feeling its bite as I squashed it. A flying worm, recently hatched by the looks of it. A tiny mark on my flesh revealed the baby bug's desperation to hold on to life. There's a rumour, started by a competitor, that my vaccine does not offer protection from their venom.

The sting as I injected myself into the red bite reminded me I am alive. Like it says on the packet, you can't be too *Safe*.

Annoyed with myself for touching the insect, I threw Ice's perfume at the mirror. The bottle smashed, the mirror remained intact. How would I have explained a crack in the mirror to her of all people?

I knew before checking that there would be nothing unusual on the snooper today. No secret signal, no clue. But I looked anyway.

Rewind. Erase myself smashing the bottle. Rewind further. See myself leave in the morning. Slavia cleaning as programmed in a floral apron, reminiscent of a mother in a nostalgic picture book. Ice's idea: a nice touch.

Or is it sinister? She never talks about her past. Does she love her parents too much to talk about them? Or, like me, is she concealing something?

Slavia switches on the other machines, observing as they silently clean the kitchen. Obeying orders requires a lack of subtlety. Simple people are despised while machines are valued for their lack of ambiguity.

'Why did you call her Slavia?' I asked Ice.

It's just a name.

My quest for secret signs, hidden meanings, annoys her.

Fast forward too far. Rewind. Find the bit I want. Ice's sleepy yawn as she wakes, stretches, throws back the quilt revealing naked flesh. She knows I am watching. It is a performance. But every time it seems real.

Check again. Expect nothing. Find nothing. A feeling I have missed something. Search again. Nothing except what I always see, my beautiful wife bathing. Carefully cleansing the flesh I cannot see below the blanket of bubbles. Drying herself with a white towel, discarding it on the floor. Standing naked at the mirror as she puts in the silver eyes. Stepping into her hand-stitched silk underwear, slim white legs extended in turn. Her perfection shames me.

Where does she go all day? What does she do? Who does she meet?

After we married, I stopped following her. Coveting something I already possessed was humiliating. But I kept tracks on her. To keep her safe. The earrings she never takes off reveal her location. I could track her now.

What if you don't like what you find?

The signal is strong and steady like her heart, beating on relentlessly. Is she close to the border? In the bar where her friend Maybella works? I only have to push the button. Then I will know.

Is she meeting someone? Mr S Graham? Why not

go to his office? I can't picture Mr S Graham tapping his foot to the old jukebox's tunes.

Ice never answers her telephone but sometimes she calls me.

Darling, I'll be home soon. Maybella is depressed again. Couldn't get away.

But she will not call; not tonight. Her phone is in my hand, staring up at me.

I could go to the bar, risk looking needy like that night she caught me waiting outside.

'Spying on me?'

'I was just passing.'

She laughed, apparently unconcerned that I had seen her sitting too close to the bad boy in the bar. Heads almost touching. Was she giggling? And him showing off for her, a cruel smile on his full lips. Is that her type? A young black boy with an uncertain future?

I should have hired someone to follow her.

Mr S Graham is bound to have a snoop on his payroll. Then Ice would be safe. She would be home. I would not be here alone waiting for my world to change forever.

I've been rehearsing this moment since we met. The moment when I know I have lost her. But I do not really believe she is gone. She will come in any minute. I will hear her footsteps cross the iron bridge. She dislikes being ferried across the water by Rob. And I adore the click click of her heels, mimicking the beating of my heart as she catwalks closer.

All I have to do is wait.

The first time I saw her I knew without even having the thought: *she's the one.*

The elevator doors opened and she was there. Wearing a scarlet sundress that would be vulgar on any other woman. Shoes a little too high. No perfume; just the unique scent of her skin.

I realised immediately that she could not afford jewels. Something I could give her. Her blue-white skin a brilliant setting for any stone.

She was going up.

I had come down.

I went back up.

The sexual intimacy of an elevator ride is cheapened by its portrayal in trashy movies, but being in that lift with Ice felt like something holy. She's going to the top floor, the rooftop restaurant, the sky's not the limit.

It hadn't occurred to me to fall in love. I wasn't the kind of male who fantasised about meeting a beautiful stranger and escaping my workaholic life. I was happy – or thought I was happy – being serviced twice a week at the germ-free.

Before Fleshworld took over there were a few sex caves on this side, though not many men used them. Sex was already dangerous though not yet prohibited.

The extortionate cost and fear of being reported made the germ-frees unpopular.

Younger women weren't going into prostitution here, so it was a job left to flesh grannies who had passed a test in male masturbation. Their wizened hands had, after all, years of practice behind them.

Maybe I felt undeserving of beauty, with my sex scar and fear of love. Maybe I felt that leathery flesh performing a chore for payment was all a man like me deserved.

I didn't think this out loud. It was a feeling rather than a thought. I didn't lie awake at night promising I'd never allow a woman to hurt me again. Mother was the furthest thing from my mind in those days.

Seeing Ice changed my life.

That's the name I gave her. Standing side by side in the lift, aware of the fine hairs on her upper arm. The forearm was smooth. She must have saved up and had it lasered, the fashion at the time. Immediately I fell in love with that remaining fine down.

She stayed silent and still, while the amplified beating of my heart gave me away. Tears leaked from the corner of my right eye. An allergic reaction, perhaps to the cheap fabric of her dress in an airless space. Newly rich, I wore only silks and cashmere. Addicted to the best in everything, I sensed her approval of my suit at least.

She glanced at me before stepping out of the lift into the rooftop restaurant. Or did she glance not at me but at her own reflection in the mirrored wall?

I waited until she walked to the corner table, watching her friend, an excitable woman in a turquoise suit, stand to greet her. Animation wears out a face. Ice has a serene face, untroubled by excess emotion.

I waited in my car until she emerged, alone, at half past nine.

I followed her home, made a note of her address, and started sending presents. Giving her things is something I am good at.

The way I met her. Casual. Chance.

Was it a plot to relieve me of my fortune? Did Mr S Graham put her in my path?

How could it be? I went to the restaurant on impulse. I had never been there before. Nobody knew I was going there. I did not even know myself until I stopped my car and went in.

You were being followed.

That is crazy. Ice was there first.

They are in it together.

Normally I suppress Mother's voice. But tonight I am listening, egging her on to fuel my paranoia.

On the periphery of my vision, on the security screen, I could see a red alert flashing. Big news. Danger. Doom.

Chairman Luck is losing too many flesh girls. Escaping to freedom on the other side where they die of cold instead of sex decay, if they make it across the black hole.

Where is my wife?

Opening her legs for men.

I don't want to look at the tracker. Don't want to know. Not yet. I have to do something.

What?

I called the bar, hanging up without leaving a message. Maybella is not working tonight.

It is not possible. Ice has not left me. She has been taken. Kidnapped. Prevented from coming home. Until I know for sure that I have lost her, it is possible to alter the outcome.

Any minute now, I will get the call. Telling me how much they want for her. I'd pay everything I have to get her back. Then, penniless, I'd lose her.

During my panic, I am still listening for her footsteps on the iron bridge, crossing the water, tapping closer to me.

Darling, I'm home.

She will walk in, almost smiling.

Nothing today.

She has everything already. Why does she even go shopping? She always comes home empty-handed.

Kissing me lightly. *Maybella wouldn't shut up.*

Yes, she is probably with her friend. Drinking coffee in that rooftop restaurant she likes so much, where I first saw her, with its expensive cocktails and hazy view of Fleshworld. Once, in an unguarded moment, she told me she likes being up high in case she decides to jump.

But Ice isn't the type for suicide. She'd more likely push someone off the roof than jump.

I adjust the colour of the lake from grey to the serene green she likes. Add a few ducks. No, swans. Ice doesn't like ducks. Put on the retro compilation Ice sings along to in the car. Prepare the bubble for her entrance. She's sure to be home soon.

Staring out of the glass wall of the bubble at the stagnant water surrounding our home, music older than Mother fills the silence.

This used to be a park, full of birds and laughter, close to the home of prime ministers past. Centuries before that, after the reign of the dinosaurs but lifetimes before the current pestilence, there was a leper hospital on this site. The park was named after it.

Did the lepers float on the lake, singing softly as they fed the birds? Now the birds are dead, but the trees are still here. The new city is the same but different, populated with old people, safe in their fortresses, and feral children roaming in search of food and fun.

Rob and his robot sons round up the lost ones if they come too close. Ice has a game where she pretends Rob, our security guard, is secretly in love with Slavia. Why can't machines fall in love?

Suspended in the present tense, with no link to the past or future, distracting myself. Nothing bad can happen while I'm in the continuous present staring at the water.

When I start the tracker, this becomes real. Before I push the button, she could still walk in.

Act like nothing's happened.

Isn't that what we're taught to do? Say nothing, do nothing. Let's pretend, happy end.

Her vampire smile. Her sleeping limbs. My little fears. My fairground lies. My ancient wound. A message from the past, impossible to read in the present.

I'm losing my mind. Thinking in song lyrics. Aware of something I am not ready to acknowledge.

Her stilettos are tapping their way towards me. I recognise her step. But our security system isn't reacting to the sound. I'm hearing what I long to hear.

Tap Tap Tap.

Wouldn't it be nice?

A cat appeared on my snooper. Cats are illegal now. They have too many diseases. *Safe* only works on people.

Mother had an orange cat called Saturn. Her bad-tempered beast was useful for killing smaller animals. He ignored me and I ignored him.

My friend Helvetia had a dog. Chairman Luck rounded up the dogs and put them to work. But people had pets back then. They took them to parks to run and play. Trees had leaves. The world looked different.

It wasn't just that. It was different. I felt different. Inside. I was softer. Sadder. I used to cry silently under the bedclothes. I had a different name.

Richard does not cry. Rich would track down the thing he had lost and bring it home.

I have to save her.

What are you waiting for?

I picked up the tracker, holding my breath.

You're scared.

Has she been suddenly overcome by fever in a crowded place? She wakes up sweating in the night, sometimes crying. It is forgotten by morning. Not forgotten; not mentioned.

I looked again at the snooper. There she is, injecting her thigh with *Safe*.

I need to know what happened. I need to find her.

The Dirty House

Killing the cat was my first mistake.

Close up it looked nothing like Saturn, nothing to do with Mother. Petty cruelty leaks out of me sometimes, making me ashamed. I didn't need to mutilate it. I should have zapped it and left its remains for Beast Patrol. But using my bare hands for the kill was strangely satisfying.

I took another dose of *Safe,* injecting myself quickly in the neck. Seven empty vials of *Safe* are lined up on the counter. How could I have missed that? Did she leave them out as a clue. Is she planning to be gone for a week? Or did she just forget to bin them?

I have seven days to find her. Six days. Today is almost over. After that, she is no longer safe.

She's gone for a week of sin.

When the Dirties arrived, I was still cleaning blood off my hands. Stains in the crevices of my dry skin distress me. Each time it happens I imagine it will be impossible to wash them clean.

'I am sorry, sir. You will have to come in for testing.'

Confusion enclosed the big flat faces, magnified on my screen. I am the man who invented *Safe*. Why would I risk myself killing something with my bare hands?

They stepped closer to the bridge but stopped; uncertain. Rob's human features are disconcerting.

'Do you know who I am?' My voice sounded pompous, disturbing the silence of the night.

'Mr Richard Powers, sir.' Their odour was unclean. Even at this distance, I could smell decay.

'I invented *Safe*.'

'Everyone must comply, sir. We have to take you in for testing.'

'I am safe.'

'You must follow the rules, sir.'

'I made the fucking rules, you mong.'

'That is insulting, sir.'

I disabled Rob and went out on to the deck to talk to them, intending to offer a bribe before realising they are not human. Their faces, close-up, are almost as convincing as Rob's. I wonder who made them?

'I can't go with you now. It's my wife.'

'Your wife?'

'She's missing.'

'How do you know she's missing…sir?'

'Because she is not here.'

An impulse to destroy them flooded my senses; almost a sexual thrill. I could shove them into the water. Damage their innards.

'Is that her blood, sir?'

'There was a cat...'

'There are no cats in Pure World, sir.'

That is the party line of course.

'Don't be ridiculous. The cat is why you are here.'

He stared at the blood on my hands.

'There it is...'

But there was no sign of a dead cat in the bushes, only the dirty face of a small child spying on me. Can't have been there long; Rob would have sniffed it out.

'Look, I have to find my wife.'

'I am sorry, sir. We have to follow orders.'

'I invented the vaccine and if you don't...'

I was sheeted and in the transit before I could finish my threat.

They took me to headquarters and extracted a sample.

They will have to let me out when it comes back clean. In Fleshworld Luck's men could lock me up and throw away the code. But here at the Dirty House they have to let me go. As long as I do not give them any excuse to detain me longer.

Why don't I summon Mr S Graham? Find out what he knows. Has Ice left me?

Why now, after ten years together? Was she playing a long game, waiting for my fortune to peak? You can't tell to look at me, but I am probably the richest man in Pure World. Everyone needs to be safe.

But if she had left me Mr S Graham would have

been in touch by now. He'd have to tell me if she... wants something. *Everything*?

The clock is, literally, ticking while I aggravate my paranoia. I should be out there searching. Now I'm locked in limbo instead of tracking Ice.

Why didn't I ping the tracker straight away? Am I scared of what I will find? Scared to discover that Mother was right after all. I am impossible to love. Mother betrayed me. Why not my wife?

It was maddening, locked in that cell.

Cleaner than last time I was here. Sterile. Ashamed of its filthy past.

'You may have to wait for a while, sir,' the Dirty told me apologetically. 'Everyone is busy tonight.'

'Busy with what?' There is no crime in Pure World. The Dirty House is just a testing lab now.

'The border, sir.'

'The border?'

'Chairman Luck has closed the border, sir.'

'No one is allowed to leave Fleshworld?'

'Who goes in must come out.'

He started another apology, then allowed it to drift into an unfinished sentence. This one was real. Machines don't repeat apologies. How long has he been working here?

The door clanged behind him, like it does in vintage movies.

Who goes in must come out. A Pleasure Pass takes you in to Fleshworld and allows you to leave at the end of your slot. Fleshtrippers outstaying the value of their credits will be terminated.

Why close the border now? Is that why Ice didn't come home? Is she stuck in Fleshworld?

What's the dirty bitch doing there?

I just need to be patient. Just a little while longer. As soon as my test comes back clear, they will let me out. Then I can activate the tracker and find out where she is.

Last time I was locked up here, all was lost. It was the day the city split in two. Cold and clean on one side, hot and dirty on the other. The odds were against me, stacked up lovingly. I should never have survived.

Mother's manic laughter taunted me as I was dragged away.

'There's blood on your hands,' the Dirty told me. And that time it wasn't an animal's blood; nor was it quite human.

Everything was lost. But I was determined. Where there's a will, there's an escape route. And I have been escaping ever since into that perfect world I created with Ice.

A dream needs two players to sustain.

She has *escaped*.

No, she needs me. I can see it in her eyes, the way she looks at me when she thinks I am distracted. We are the same, her and me. Two people addicted to each other. She would never leave me. Would she?

She has no reason to want to escape, no reason at all. And people don't just disappear. A beautiful woman leaves a trail. The eyes that follow her everywhere retain an imprint. She is the last person who could become invisible.

Ashamed of the relief I would feel if she has been taken; instead of running from me.

Where is she?

Is she safe?

Imagine your worst fear. Being contaminated forever. That is what most people fear. Dying an ugly death.

I cannot bear the idea of her being corrupted with sex decay. Her beauty annihilated with disease if she does not get inoculated in time. If I don't get her back in seven days she is lost to me forever. She may as well be trapped in the flesh zone.

Has she… run away with Luck? I push this thought away, make it invisible; like Luck himself. *Run to him?*

I am being ridiculous. She doesn't know Chairman Luck. No one has ever seen him. Does he even exist?

Ice has never been to Fleshworld. She is out shopping. When I get home, she will be waiting for me, soaking in bubbles with a glass of iced vodka in her blue-white hand. She will smile at me. Everything will be all right. She will not even ask where I have been.

I lack Ice's talent. I can't make my mind go blank,

focus on the beautiful infinity of a blue diamond; a weakness in a man obsessed with being in control. The crone's voice is always in my head; refusing to be silenced.

Rage seeped out of me as I paced the cell. I know only one story that can distract me. That flawed story which I have never, properly, understood. I pushed it aside, refusing to examine it. Afraid of not managing to make sense of it, or maybe scared of finally understanding.

The Game of Boo

Memory is vindictive.

There must have been happy days. There were happy days, playing outside with Helvetia and her brother Paul, back when Pure World was called London. Fleshworld didn't even exist except maybe in Chairman Luck's imagination.

We lived near the river, where me and Helvetia and Paul swam naked on hot days. I had to be sure I was completely dry before going home or Mother would have found me out.

Their mother was always smiling. She would open the back door and offer each of us a buttery potato scone, an old recipe from her island home.

I was forbidden to enter their house. The scent of colour and laughter wafted out into the yard; tempting me. Their white dog, Wolf, licked my hand; inviting me in.

Helvetia's father was dead too, but she had a picture of him on her bedside table beside her night light. I had never seen my father. She wanted to show me the picture of hers. Maybe there would be an opportunity on Sunday, while Mother was busy with her Party cronies. They stayed all afternoon, gossiping about impure people. She disliked me getting under their feet.

Helvetia's family were often out on a Sunday. Mrs Powers had asked my mother if I could go with them to the park to enjoy coloured drinks with ice-cream floating inside the glass. But she replied, 'It is against Party rules.'

Mother's love for the Pure Party was a form of denial. It forbade everything pleasurable except the smug satisfaction she found in suppressing pleasure itself.

'Do not let me catch you enter the house of the unbeliever,' she warned me. And I took her threats seriously.

But I longed to see the photograph of Helvetia's father. I had no pictures of mine. It was forbidden to speak of him. I had no memory of him either, and saw his face in random male acquaintances.

Perhaps he looked like kind Dr Merryweather, with his silver hair and tweed suits? Or maybe more dashing, like one of the movie stars I have seen through the window on the Powers' gigantic screen. My father definitely does not resemble Mr Fletch, a Purist fanatic, who owns the mulch shop.

Mother had implied that my father looked like me. There was an insinuation of something shameful. I must have been very small, because she was bathing me. She stared at me and said, 'Just like him.'

She held me at arm's length while drying me, unwilling to witness the male part of my body.

'Cover yourself up,' she said, handing me my pyjamas and shooing me into my bedroom. Her voice was anxious, urgent.

As I bent to pull up the pyjama bottoms, she slapped me hard across the buttocks. The blow took me by surprise. I toppled, cracking my head on the bedpost. Mother snapped out the light with a chuckle.

I hid under the covers, imagining my father. Is he dark like me? I wanted to look like him. But there was no trace he had ever existed. That is what I believed. Of course I was mistaken. I was the trace, the scent, the *evidence* of him.

The violence was sporadic. A pleasure she did not allow herself every day.

At night I struggled to stay awake. To keep watch, just in case. In case of what?

Her party trick was creeping into my room and shouting Boo loud in my ear. I fell for it every time, jumping out of my sleep.

No matter how hard I tried, I could not stay awake all night. I could not do it. And she knew it.

She allowed me a cup of hot chocolate at bedtime and would sit watching me drink it, her fingers busy with sewing or sharpening the big silver scissors from her work basket.

After the full extent of her strangeness emerged, I wondered if she had drugged my drink every night?

Did she shorten the odds on the game of Boo with a dose of *Sleep*? The sweet, sticky hot chocolate would surely have been forbidden; unless it was a beard for her true purpose?

I knew I would pay for going into Helvetia's bedroom but the invitation was tempting.

On Sunday afternoon it was raining. I had been told to wait in the yard until the Purists departed. Mrs Powers saw me and beckoned, silently, with a wave of her hand.

She opened the back door, ushering me inside. 'You'll catch your death,' she said when we were safe in the kitchen.

She gave me one of Paul's shirts to wear while mine was drying by the fire. Helvetia and Paul were watching the end of a movie. I was almost afraid to look directly at the screen in case I would betray signs of it later. Could the pictures somehow brand me, alerting mother to my voyeurism?

After the film, Helvetia took my hand and we went upstairs together. Her mother didn't so much as glance in our direction as we left the room.

Helvetia's bedroom was painted pink and full of dolls. My eyes went straight to the photograph of her handsome father. He looked like Paul, and this gave me hope of resembling my own father.

Helvetia lay on her bed chewing gum.

'What shall we do now?'

I wasn't sure how to answer.

'Are you madly in love with me?'

'Of course.'

This was one of our routines, normally played outdoors under the trees.

'Well then,' she said, getting daring, 'you'd better show me your thing.'

She wasn't serious. She broke down in peals of laughter. I joined her on the bed and we lay there giggling. She didn't really want to see my sex tool.

I learned later that Rottweiler, mother's name for the male organ, is a breed of dog. But I teased Helvetia, saying, 'Rottie is coming to get you.' And she laughed harder and harder.

Suddenly Mother was standing in the doorway staring at us.

'Where is your shirt?' she asked coldly.

She waited until after dinner then beat me with her royal blue Sunday shoe.

Unusually for her, the special shoes had a little pointy heel. She used this to beat me about the head, careful not to hit the same spot twice. She prefers not to leave a mark. But sometimes it is unavoidable.

That was the first time she had used an instrument other than her hands. A shoe cannot quite be classed as a weapon. It has another function. But she wielded it like a dagger, and I fell to the ground. As a parting insult, she kicked me hard in the back while I was balled up in pain.

Mrs Powers noticed next day that I was walking funny. She asked if I was all right.

'Yes,' I lied.

I had a stitch in my side. But it wasn't that bad. Complaining wouldn't get me anywhere.

Mrs Powers waited until Mother had left for work and took me to Dr Merryweather. His surgery was on the corner, and we could get in and out quickly without being seen.

The receptionist assumed that Mrs Powers was my mother, and we did not correct her. Dr Merryweather knew me by sight though I was not a patient at his surgery. I kept my eyes closed while he examined me. He asked me where it hurt. I pointed; hoping they could not see the blood soiling my underpants. I'd be in trouble for that later.

They exchanged glances a few times and then we left. I felt happy, walking along with Mrs Powers. My pleasure was diluted with fear we had been seen coming out of the sweet shop. She bought me rainbow sherbert to eat now and a bag of treats to share with Helvetia and Paul.

Dr Merryweather knocked on our door later. He spoke to Mother alone in the parlour. I was too frightened to listen at the keyhole. We were not his patients. Why was he here? When he left, she would stand me naked before her and accuse me.

Mother showed him out, face tight with rage, but said nothing to me. I waited for her to act. All night I held my breath. But nothing happened that night.

After Dr Merryweather's visit, she confined herself

to discreet shakes.

Holding me by the shoulders, she shook me until I rattled. I enjoyed being shook but was careful not to let this show.

There was never a mark on me, until the scissors. Maybe it was holding back for so long that made her final attack so vicious?

Her pleasure in holding the scissors was obvious. She worked with them after supping, unable to keep her fingers still. Stitching, mending. 'My work never ends,' she said with satisfaction.

The needles in her basket glinted at me as I sipped my hot chocolate. The shades of thread, black and grey like our clothes, did not appeal to me.

On impulse, I tipped my hot chocolate into her prickly plant while she was distracted by her scissors. Was that the trigger that set the events in motion? If I had drunk the chocolate and went to sleep, would she never have been provoked into the attack?

No. Some other excuse would have arisen, later or sooner. She enjoyed tidying up too much ever to leave loose ends.

I lay with my eyes tight shut, waiting for her to come in and give me a fright.

I had not planned ahead. I didn't know what I would do when she screamed Boo in my ear. Jump as usual, feigning surprise? Or give her a superior smile that would warn her the joke was cold.

I fantasised about saying, 'The laugh is on you

tonight, Mother.' But I had no talent for answering back.

Maybe I did drift off for a bit.

I became aware of voices downstairs. Mother's voice, and a man's. With the mad logic of a child, I became convinced that the man must be my father. Why else would a strange man be in the house in the middle of the night?

My father. Come to collect me. Taking me away from here at last.

Excited, I ran downstairs.

As I approached the parlour door, I became more cautious. Now I could not hear the voices but I knew that they were in there.

I was scared. I wanted to go back. But what if she told my father I didn't want to see him? She was not above telling lies if they protected her reputation with the Pure Party. The Party is Mother's religion, sanctioning vengeance and hate.

I have to be brave. I cannot lose this chance to see my father. I may never get another opportunity.

Careful not to creak, I pushed open the door.

This cannot be possible.

Mother lay on the sofa, almost concealed beneath a large man. Her skirt had ridden up revealing the bare flesh at the tops of her stockings. It reminded me of chicken skin before it is cooked.

A look of fury overcame her. She closed the gap between us with one leap, beating me with her fists. 'Spying on me!'

'Don't be silly, Mona,' the man said, trying to make light of her mad turn. 'The boy won't remember any of this in the morning.'

The man, who is Mr Fletch from the mulch shop, winked at me saying, 'Go back to bed, boy.'

I should have run then. I should have run next door to Mrs Powers, who told me to tell her straight away if Mother ever hurt me again. Run all the way to the ocean. Kept on and on running until I reached Utopia; the island with safe sunshine and no diseases where Mrs Powers grew up.

But no. I went back upstairs and waited for the consequences. I expected a beating, something along the lines of what I had received after being caught in Helvetia's bedroom wearing someone else's shirt.

Maybe more severe, but minus the kick in the kidneys at the end. Dr Merryweather's visit had scared her. Helvetia told me he had looked inside me and found Mother's mark. She would not want to cause internal bleeding again and risk the wrath of Dr Merryweather.

That's what I thought, lying there in the dark, listening to Mr Fletch take his leave. There were whispers at the back door, then I heard her go into the parlour. Probably tidying the cushions, removing traces of his visit.

But no. She left the clearing up that night. She had a more pressing task to deal with.

The moon, entering through the stair window, lit her from behind as she came at me in my bedroom.

Was she smiling? Or is it the sharp smile of the scissors I remember?

The scissors shone as they closed in on me. Surely she wasn't going to sew the button back on my pyjamas at this time of night? She had noticed it loose at bedtime and been irritated by the sight of it dangling, but was in too much of a hurry to fix it.

'What do you want?'

Mother continued her chant as she closed in on my bed. Not a prayer. A mantra? No, an instruction; repeated to reinforce intent.

Snip off your sin. Snip off your sin.

The scissors stabbed at my groin, first ripping the cotton then the skin. She was stronger than me but my blood gushing forth repulsed her; creating a pause. I managed to punch her hard in her female area. She doubled over, dropping her weapon as she clutched her receptacle in pain.

'Evil boy,' she screamed, as I ran out of my room.

Ignoring the blood running down my legs, I jumped downstairs four at a time; managing not to fall. She stumbled after me, the twin blades of her scissors snipping open and shut onto air.

Snip off your sin. Snip off your sin.

The door was locked. I tried to break the window

with my fist. I was screaming.

Miraculously, she slipped on the trail of blood I had left on the stairs, cracking her head open on the stone steps.

Saturn lapped up my blood as I crawled through the animal flap. I was worried that Mother would regain consciousness and come at me again with the scissors. I do not know how long it took me to wriggle through the flap to the freedom of the yard. Longer than it may have done if I had not been intent on keeping my sex tool protected, pressed hard against the cold floor until the last minute; lessening the time when she could close in with the twin blades and complete her work.

But she was out cold. And so was I by the time I had crawled next door to Mrs Powers.

'You are a lucky boy,' the doctor told me next day.

It was not Dr Merryweather. I was in the Hospital of Hope and the damage had been assessed. I would not lose my organ as Mother had intended.

'There will be a scar,' the doctor informed Mrs Powers, who had watched over me in the night. I wondered who was looking after Helvetia and Paul and had a few anxious moments until she saw my distress and assured me they were safe. 'Most of its functions will remain unaffected,' the doctor continued brightly.

He did not spell it out. But I am unable to breed. There is no seed inside me.

'The scar will be concealed beneath his sex hair when he is older.'

And it is. Hair does not grow on scar tissue but it grows around it. Scar tissue never really heals.

When I came out of hospital, I had four years in the House of Abandon. The other children hated it, but it was Heaven for me. They dreamed of being claimed by a lost parent; while I dreaded it.

Every night in the dark I failed to fall asleep; certain she would come for me. Eventually she did.

'Number 404, your mother is here,' Matron Correction said.

Mother stood with her arms folded, a grin cracking open her face.

Our story was not over yet.

Mother's lunacy had been caused by revulsion at growing the male sex organ inside her. She was cured with a series of shock treatments and unhappy pills in the House of Despair.

Now that she had admitted the terror of her ways and promised not to castrate me; she was deemed fit to look after a child. She never sewed again. The temptation to cut me would have been too great if she had been allowed to touch the implements secured in her sewing basket. Evil was hiding inside her, waiting for an outlet.

Has her cruelty been breeding in me since

childhood? Has Ice seen it lurking behind my tight lips as I pretend to sleep? Did that make her leave me?

On the first night of our reunion, I made it clear to Mother that the power had shifted. I was not taking orders from her anymore. She was no longer in a position to threaten me with violence.

To make my point, I sat down and sewed a button on to my school uniform. Taking pleasure in the slow progress of the needle, I felt her eyes on me.

She watched in silence. Unable to leave the room, unable to take her eyes off the shiny new scissors I had bought to taunt her. Her old face was slack with emotion, lust even; anticipating the quick, sharp snip of the scissors at the end of my task.

When I had finished taunting Mother, I locked up the scissors and went next door to see Helvetia and her family. But they had gone. Moved back home, the man who answered their door told me.

Mrs Powers had wanted to return to her island birthplace ever since her husband died, but had to save up for transit passes. I knew they would be happy there. In memory of their kindness, and because I preferred not to share Mother's surname, I changed my name to Richard Powers.

I started saving up myself. As soon as it was legally permitted, I left home. Living first in a room, and later in a large apartment. By the time I met Ice I had my own house.

We selected the bubble together, a safe place to protect us from intruders; except those we take inside ourselves.

But my question to myself, the one I have never answered, is this. After escaping from Mother, why did I go back? Why did I maintain contact with her? She had tried to cut off my organ and there I was giving her money and visiting once a year on her birthday.

She resented my financial assistance but took it anyway, her gnarled paw stroking the banknotes. I should have known she was not finished with me.

But what did I want from her? News of my father? Why would I expect her to reward me with that after years of denying his existence? The little I know about him I found out at my trial.

But why was I foolish enough to expect anything from her except further punishment? In retrospect, it is easy to see how she set me up. At the time I really did not see it coming.

The sad truth is that I wanted some sign from her. I longed for love to fill the hole inside. I knew it would never come. That did not stop me wanting it.

Emotional weakness caused me to lower my guard, imagining I knew all her tricks, pretending she could cause me no more pain. It was my turn to make her suffer.

Was the plan forming already in my mind? Was I building up to that evil act? Was it my intention all along to steal her soul?

Suddenly, Mother was old.

She had already surpassed the life expectancy of her class, living on malice. But she had a rancid odour; her flesh was decaying. She looked dirty despite her frequent baths; scrubbing at her thin skin with a pumice stone. And she had taken to walking into doors and falling off stools, giving herself black eyes and broken limbs.

'Why couldn't you have died instead of your sister?' she asked repeatedly; becoming a bore on the subject. After her death I discovered that this sister had never existed. A dead twin was cut out of Mother minutes before I was born, but he was male.

My father existed. Hope welled up in me when his name was mentioned at my trial. That old fantasy of him appearing to rescue me had never really died.

But father was just another humiliating detail in my story. He had expired from sex decay. My father, the hero, was a sex leper. Too poor to be inoculated; he had literally fucked himself to death.

I had to stand in the dock every day, listening to horrible stories about my own past. I was almost glad when Judge Dark sentenced me. At least I didn't have to hear anything more about motive, how my inherited lunacy had provoked me to rape and murder Mother. That was the final assault. The last humiliation she visited on me from beyond the incinerator.

I couldn't figure it out, lying in my cell, worrying over this hideous new detail. But of course. The knitting needles. She must have used one of those to tear her rectum.

But I'm getting ahead of myself. Cheating, in fact. Trying to jump cut to the trial to avoid the really horrible bit.

When I visited Mother on her birthday, she had another black eye.

I'd assumed that her accidents were on account of her age. Could I have been expected to know that these injuries were all part of the plan? These marks on her old flesh, which she photographed religiously, were intended to incriminate me. How could I not have guessed?

But on her half-century, I was distracted by pride in my growing success. I wanted to shame her with a really expensive gift. She had never celebrated my birthday, and would be affronted by a present.

It was a chore figuring out what to buy her. Jewellery didn't seem offensive enough. A crate of champagne was asking for trouble, providing her with bottles to throw at me.

Browsing in the Wishing Well, admiring recreations of luxury vintage that I could easily afford, my nose took me to the shoe department and its scent of leather. Ladies seated elegantly on low flesh-pink velvet stools, assisted by girls in tailored, white coats, tried on shoe after shoe before making a final sensual selection. They stretched out their legs, admiring their purchases, offering me an opportunity to compare their ankles. I can afford a woman like that now. The thought took me by surprise.

'Can I help you, sir?' one of the young assistants asked flirtatiously. Has my fortune marked me? Made me a target for greedy girls? Or is she just gale-force friendly with everyone?

I explained what I was looking for. We had to guess Mother's size. But that did not matter, as she was unlikely ever to wear the shoes.

I arrived at her house, my expensive present elaborately wrapped in cloth of gold and tied with bows, to be greeted by a posse of Purists.

Surely she isn't having a party? Well, anything is possible.

But there was no party. Her cronies were there to admonish me.

'This will have to stop,' one of them said, kicking things off.

'You cannot treat an elder like this,' Mrs Fletch hissed, spitting on me. Her husband stood behind her, bent and silent.

'Evil cur,' an old man shouted in my ear, setting about me with his stick. 'After all she has done for you.'

'Devil's spawn,' they chanted together. Well, I never did like Happy Birthday. What's happy about decaying, year after year? And if I am the devil's bastard, what does that make Mother?

She sat in the corner, cackling with indecent pleasure. She had trumped me again. The surprise of the royal blue stilettos, waiting in their box, palled in comparison to this reception.

Evidently Mother, who appeared to have a sense of humour after all, had reported me for beating her. On closer inspection, she had a deep gash on her balding head to go with the usual black eye and cut lip. But no broken limbs this time.

I didn't take their accusations seriously. I should have. But I laughed them off. I was as yet unaware of her grand finale. I thought this was her party trick; instead it was just the warm-up act. She was stocking up witnesses against me, and each one of the Purists took delight in testifying at my trial.

They were so clearly mad, how could I have known Judge Dark would believe them? And how could anyone, even me, have predicted how far she would actually go?

I presented her with the shoes, and took my leave of the party, promising to return the next night with fuel. She had refused my offer of a digital heating system, insisting on keeping her old-fashioned furnace.

I arrived at eight as agreed, letting myself in with the key under the mat.

'I have nothing to hide,' she said, when I'd offered to upgrade her security.

To my surprise, she had unwrapped the blue shoes and placed them on the mantelpiece.

I stood at the bottom of the stairs, calling her. I could not bring myself to shout, 'Mother.' So I made do with, 'Hello, you up there?'

No response.

I walked slowly upstairs.

I had rarely been upstairs since leaving home. I never used the bathroom on my visits, and had too many unpleasant memories of my bedroom to take a nostalgic turn in there.

Snip off your sin. Snip off your sin.

Mother wasn't in her room.

The television was on. I installed it for her last birthday, high on the wall opposite her bed, tempting her to disobey the Party. Her snout was always glued to trash, sound muted in case snoopers caught her in the act.

Surely she has not gone out? That would be just like her, having insisted I come tonight with the fuel.

'Eight sharp,' she'd warned me. She claimed to be desperate for it.

But where would she have gone? She only leaves the house to go to Pure Party meetings. And it's past her bedtime already. That fact alone should have been enough to warn me.

On impulse, I pushed open the bathroom door with my foot.

I should never have gone in there. If I hadn't touched her, it would have been more difficult for them to pin her mutilation on me.

The accusations of my cruelty and the crew of old witnesses would still have been in place. But that lacks the force of hard physical evidence.

I should have walked away, left her displayed there. Instead I provided the Dirty Patrol with a wealth of DNA evidence against myself. I helped her to convict me.

Mother was lying in a bathtub of blood, legs splayed open, her ankles tied to the hot and cold taps.

Her hands were less tightly tied behind her head. The razor which had hacked her open was washed and neatly replaced on the shelf. There was not a trickle of blood on it.

The razor was what gave her away. If at first glance I'd assumed that she'd been murdered, the detail of the clean razor convinced me this was her work.

A psychotic intruder would not replace the razor on the shelf. Mother definitely would. It was ingenious. Who other than me would believe that she could slash herself then wash up before bleeding to death in the bathtub?

But this didn't occur to me at the time.

It was later, with plenty of opportunity for reflection, that I figured out the details. That night I went into a panic.

My first instinct was to try to revive her, even

though she was clearly dead. I was terrified of seeing her pubic hair again. The night I surprised her fornicating on the sofa with Mr Fletch, I had caught a glimpse of it as she leapt at me. It was thick and dark in those days.

I turned my face from the body in the bath, catching my own shadow on the moonlit window.

If I had examined closely, I would have seen the mess of her female parts; hacked open to reveal a deeper, bloody hole. Mother had cut off her own cunt.

Her legs had been tied with male underpants. The pants had been hacked up with scissors to make them effective as binds. Of course they were mine.

Not mine exactly, not ones I had worn, but they had my name on them. When I saw my name embroidered on the crotch, I understood her reference. That pushed me over the edge into a mood of both fury and panic, as she knew it would.

The scarred area on my genitals started its ritual throb. My sex scar will be with me forever; a daily reminder that my mother tried to unman me with a big pair of scissors.

One of her eyes was open, watching me. Was she still alive? Had she timed it just right, so she would see my shame and disgust one last time?

Untying her, I knocked a jar of witch's brew into the tub. The glass smashed, its shards sticking into her sinful parts. I had to pick them off the saggy flesh, further wrinkled by its saturation in bloody water. By the time I'd finished, she looked like she had taken a bath in broken glass.

Wrapping her clumsily in a towel, I carried her into the bedroom and covered her up. This put the nail in my coffin at the trial. When asked why I did this, I could not answer.

I wanted to cover her up. To put her somewhere I could not see her. To hide her.

Cover that thing up.

Why didn't I leave her in the bathtub and walk out the door?

Richard Powers would have done that. Of course Richard was there too. He had to do one last thing while there was the opportunity.

But Mother had managed to turn him back into the boy victim.

She didn't just want to kill herself and frame me for the murder. She wanted to destroy me. And she needed me to know that at last she had won.

The Purists condemned me with one voice at the trial. 'Mona obeyed the Pure Party's teachings. She feared her son. He is not a believer.'

Mona. How appropriate. Moaning Mona. I'd been in battle with her sadistic, thwarting will since childhood. The Pure Party are not actually for anything. They are against happiness. Mona took orgasmic pleasure in the pain of others.

Is her evil breeding in me; a killer virus hidden from sight but diminishing me just the same?

The Purists hissed at me from their seats in the public gallery, a demented chorus.

I was found guilty and sentenced to incineration.

Confined in the cell, waiting for the end, filled me with doubt.

Was I guilty of something after all? Guilty of *everything*? I'd wanted to kill her. Did I kill her?

Is that why I continued to visit Mother? Is that why I never completely broke free? I allowed her to goad me into matricide?

It's what we both wanted.

Of course. I had wanted her dead since my childhood. I fantasised about it for years.

If she was late returning home in the evening, I imagined her spattered on the track in a fatal accident. I longed for a machine to fall on her, mangling her dried-up body, in the factory where she worked; one of only a few humans bossed about by robots.

Or maybe she would drop dead of a heart attack. That happens. Helvetia's father died suddenly. Mother might choke on bile in her sleep.

Did I make the leap from fantasy to butchering my mother in her own bathtub? Somewhere, hidden from my sight, is there another Rich who does things that I am scared to?

This was my state of mind when Mr S Graham came to see me.

He was a minor member of my legal team. I'd seen him at the trial passing envelopes to the more important advocate.

Mr S Graham had a proposal for me. He considered my chances at appeal much stronger. In those days, everyone sentenced to death had automatic right of appeal.

The Dirties, he implied, without ever actually making a promise, could be bribed to lose that damning evidence. The DNA I had left behind with the crone's corpse. If they were to discover what I'd taken, even Satan's powers could not save me.

It was essential for me to grant Mr S Graham power of attorney, so that the necessary funds could be released.

'And of course, sir, your criminal record will be erased. Like it never existed. You need have no fear of it coming back to taunt you.'

That part of his plot appealed to me. The destruction of my humiliating past, that was worth paying for. Of course I knew that Mr S Graham would clean me out.

But what use was my fortune to me now? This charade was the only chance I had. Could I trust him to keep his end of the bargain? Risk me coming after him when I get out?

Possibly not. You can't trust anyone. But Mr S Graham was the only person making me an offer. I may as well take it. I had nothing, except my life, left to lose.

Justice is expensive.

But it prevails in the end. The evidence was

contaminated as it travelled to court. Corruption was not suspected; the bungling Dirties lose things all the time.

The witnesses against me had died, or been disposed of, by the time of my second trial. Mother's cronies had joined her in Hell. And I was a free man; free to make a new fortune. I had the strength to start again. I had an idea, and an ingredient for my formula which I believed would ensure its success.

I turned a blind eye to Mr S Graham's greed. He knew too much about me. Knowledge protected him.

My fortune had saved me from death. That was the lesson I learned. I was determined to make myself impregnable. My last battle with Mother led to my best-seller *Safe*.

Nothing could touch me until I fell in love with Ice. Loving her made me vulnerable; fear of losing her weakened my ruthless heart.

And now I have lost her.

City Morgue

I was standing when the Dirty opened the door, prepared to exit into the icy night and ping the tracker; to face whatever I find.

'Not so fast, sir.'

Does he know? No. It is not possible. Nobody knows. Nobody can know. My last visit here no longer exists. I paid enough to have my record erased.

'We have found your wife.'

'Where is she?'

'Here.' He motioned me to walk ahead of him along the corridor.

'Where did you find her?'

He did not respond. Did he hear me?

My heart thudded; embarrassed to be reunited with her in front of him. Emotion cheapens when witnessed.

But I couldn't hide my feeling of relief and joy and something else. It was written all over my face. What was it? Something familiar…something…

We reached the end of the corridor. A closed

steel door barred the way. As he pushed it open, I recognised the emotion I'd been struggling to name. Fear.

I saw her body straight away.

'No...'

Ignoring my distress, he pushed me towards the open drawer. I was close enough to see her pale hair seeping from its plastic cover.

'Your wife?' he asked, exposing the blue tint to her smooth dead flesh as he stripped back its wrapping. A smile loitered at the edges of her lips; the way Ice looks when she anticipates pleasure.

A high-pitched sob came out of me. The sound was almost feminine. I was unable to suppress it.

It isn't her. The same age and height and colouring. But the dead woman is not my wife.

I caught sight of myself on the snooper as I left the Dirty House, surprised by the frizz in my hair.

I pressed the tracker. Its red light throbbed, mocking my heartbeat; but failed to move. I switched off the device. Waited as long as my nerves could tolerate, switched it back on. No movement. Nothing. Either she is dead or...

She has taken off her earrings.

Should I go straight to the bar near the border, the place I saw her with that boy called Bad? Or go back to the bubble first for my jeep and some supplies. The kind of thing you need to hunt someone. A zapper in case of resistance, a bag of jewels for bribes. I should change clothes too. Wear something military. I will not be taken seriously as a hunter in a business suit.

Inside I am secretly hoping Ice will be home, waiting.

'Taxi, sir?' a voice asked, interrupting my fantasy.

In the flashlight of a drone, I noticed that the taxi driver's a sex leper. He has the mark between his eyes to indicate his organ has fallen off already. He's no longer a threat, whether he can afford to be inoculated or not.

'No,' I said. 'I'm waiting for someone.' Why the excuse? I'm allowed to say no if I want to.

He came closer and whispered, 'I know where she is.' Did I imagine it? Did he really say that? I climbed into the car.

There is no affliction worse than hope.

Passive in the back seat, I allowed the leper to drive me around in circles all night. Falling for his promise we would find the place 'they' had hidden her, soon. At the next corner he'd recognise the alleyway. Always the next corner. And me believing what I wanted to hear, was too tired to resist.

Until dawn when he stopped pretending and drove me home. I could have refused to pay the massive fare. But I couldn't waste more time arguing.

I changed into my combat gear and drove straight to the bar by the border. Most of these joints have been closed down, but some filth seeps over the edge for people who can't afford a Pleasure Pass to the other side.

But the lights were out in Paradise Alley. If Ice had been here, she was gone now. Did she go home with him, the bad boy? Is she hiding somewhere with her friend Maybella? Hiding from what? Mother's voice spat its venom into the dark.

You.

Ice has six days left.

Six days of *Safe*. Until she needs to be injected again. There is only one thing for it. I will have to call Satan.

Six Days Left

Mr S Graham was pleased to hear from me.

'Always a pleasure to be of service, Mr Powers.'

I don't have time for self-conscious dithering, but felt deep shame as I explained my problem. Already this demon knows too much about me.

His expression betrayed nothing as I spoke. If he knew already that Ice had left me, he was hiding it well.

When I had finished he said, 'Da Cunta is the man for this.' He hesitated. 'One thing, Mr Powers...'

Hesitation is not part of his normal repertoire. It does not suit him. Recovering himself he asked, 'Are you certain the lady is still alive?'

Certain? I understood his inference. I killed my mother. Why not my wife? Am I establishing an alibi; or looking for lost property.

'No, I haven't...Yes, she is alive. Of course she is.'

'It's not a cheap service, or pleasant, but da Cunta has never failed.'

That's all I need to know. His top cunt is on the case. Ice will be back in my arms soon. And this time I will never let her go.

Too restless to sleep, I drove around all day.

Time stretched into itself as I stalked the city: cold, hungry, alone. For years I've had a clear-cut mission. Making my fortune. Selling *Safe*. Now I have a problem I can't solve and too much time to think.

Time used to feel this way, heavy and dead, before I met her. But the clock isn't moving slowly. It's ticking onwards, eating up her *Safe* time.

'We need you at home, sir,' da Cunta told me.

'If she comes home, I will be alerted.'

I threw in a phoney smile; annoyed that I need his help. I should be escaping into the electric-blue sunset with Ice, not scouring the city for her.

'It's best if you stay out of sight, sir. Let me find your love lady.' Scratching his receding chin, he smirked, 'I need a list of her paramours.'

'Her *what*?'

'Did your lady have admirers?'

'Everyone who saw her. But if you mean was she betraying me, no, she wasn't.' I keep referring to her in the past tense. A bad omen?

'The protector is the last to know.'

His Pure Party vocabulary reminded me of Mother. He has a talent for aggravating me. I can kill him when this is over. What I can't do is sit doing nothing. *Waiting*.

Five Days Left

I drove around all day. And the next night. And the next day I went back to Paradise Alley and waited until Maybella appeared behind the bar.

She claimed not to have seen Ice since we married. I know that isn't true, but let it pass.

'Dropped her old friends,' she said sourly. The excuse of a customer ended our conversation.

'Has Juicy Loose been in tonight?' I heard the man asking as I disappeared into the twilight.

Sleeping alone in our bed, the bed we loved in, wasn't possible. When exhaustion was making me see double, I checked into an hotel near the border with a view of the ruins that were once the seat of parliament. But I couldn't sleep there either.

I went back to Paradise Alley and sat staring into the neon lights of Fleshworld, taunting me at the other side of the black hole. The pit of doom that appeared when the city split into two.

Before, I never understood the attraction of a Pleasure Pass to oblivion. Who needs oblivion when married to the perfect woman?

Falling in love with her made me aware of my own body. Not just my sex scar which she pretended not to see. Lumps on my flesh I'd never noticed before. Sun scars from early exposure to a harsh light which burns here no more.

When I was a boy, before the city was spliced in half, it was bright on this side too. Children played outside in the sun without protection. Sitting on the ground, in the dirt, beside old men and stray dogs, corrugating foreheads against the glare.

The skin on my face is damaged, unlike the smooth blueish tint of her complexion. Skin that's never been exposed.

Did your parents lock you up in the cellar?

I never liked the sun.

Has she left me? Did she meet a handsome man? She likes my eyes but look closely for a long time and the remains of a yellow tint can be spied behind my green lenses. A legacy left by a neglected dose of fever when I was too poor to seek treatment.

My toenails are discoloured too. I doubt if Ice ever looked at my toes.

Five days left. Five days of safety for Ice. Five days of hope left for me.

The moon was full. There was talk in the bar about eclipse night, jokes about werewolves and mad love.

The Purists believe that on a lunar eclipse the moon is shadowed to allow evil to creep into our world. On a solar eclipse, when the sun is shadowed, our hopes are corrupted. It was all about evil for Mother and her cronies.

The sun will never shine again in Pure World. The fake sun of Fleshworld is the only future for our day-dreams.

Mother did her best to murder hope. I'm thinking about her too much. I don't have time to brood. Not now the sun is permanently in shadow, not now my wife is lost.

Why did Chairman Luck close the border? Why now? Surely he wants as many visitors as possible to buy his trashy sex thrills? Controlling the numbers doesn't make sense. Unless he is hiding something. A man like that must have secrets.

Da Cunta had looked everywhere in Pure World.

'Perhaps your love lady does not want to be found.'

'Stop making excuses. Your business is finished if you fail.'

'Some free advice. Don't lose your temper.'

'I never lose my temper.'

'Almost never.'

He knows about me? That doesn't matter. I need to focus. Focus on Ice.

'There is only one place left to look.' He paused. 'If she's there, she's lost forever.'

Maybe she doesn't want to be found.

What do I know about my wife? Nothing. She has no family. Her parents died when the city was divided. That's what she told me.

'I have no past,' she said, smiling at me. And that suited me. If she had no past, I could leave my own behind and start again with her.

Increasingly, I was drawn to the border.

Did I know already she was in Fleshworld? Before I found out? Or is that just a desire to control my world by knowing everything before it happens. Control freak. Another thing I have in common with Chairman Luck.

I cannot even control my own hands, shaking and lined, as they raise a glass to my thin lips to console a thirst that will never be quenched.

At first I didn't notice the whore. I sat by the window of the bar, staring across at Fleshworld, wondering what to do.

I always have a plan. Decisions come easily to me. I am a decisive man. A man who gets what he wants.

Is my luck changing? That's stupid. It isn't luck.

What is it? Confidence? Strength? Being the one who never gives up, who lasts longer than the others?

Maybella has finished her shift. Was she telling the truth? Has she really not seen Ice? Is Ice hiding in her room?

She's the sort of woman who lives in a stuffy room with too many clothes and not enough space to hang them. She envies Ice, of course she does. Would she harm her?

A boy, slouching in the shadows at the end of the bar, caught my eye.

As he came towards me, I caught sight of her in the mirror for the first time. At first glance, I thought she was Ice.

'What's your pleasure, dude?'

The boy beckoned her to come closer and she slid off the bar stool, a surprisingly graceful movement; again reminding me of my wife.

I leaned closer, took a better look. Could he hear my heart beating inside my chest?

A sand-parched mirage. A desert vision of the face I see everywhere, now through the filter of a dusty mirror.

Of course it isn't Ice. No one could ever be her. She is the only one.

'Give the gentleman a sniff of you,' the boy said, shoving her into my sweating face.

Disturbed by this flesh girl in her pink plastic uniform, I downed my drink and left.

Four Days Left

The next night I went back to the bar, the disgusting photograph da Cunta had given me that day screwed up in my pocket.

Ordering a glass of ice water, I sat by the window. I need to keep my wits about me. For what? Still no plan.

Is that true? No. The plan was already forming, I just hadn't thought it aloud yet. Evil is something the sane shy away from. No matter how desperate. No matter how selfish.

The girl was sitting in the same corner as yesterday, forlorn like she's been there all night; unrented. She's much younger than I thought. The dress makes me gag. The same pink plastic uniform my wife has on in that picture hiding in my pocket.

Ice dressed as a flesh girl.

Selling her cunt.

It can't be her.

Da Cunta took the photograph himself. Ice in the window of a Pussy Parlour. He couldn't contain his satisfaction when he showed me.

'Flesh girl for hire.'

'You just left her there?'

'What else could I do, sir?'

'You could have snatched her.' I squeezed the vile image until my fingers were bleeding.

'I can't steal a flesh girl from under Luck's eyes.'

'There must be a way.'

'I'd be dead before I got her out of the window.'

'Nothing is impossible.'

'It is now the border has closed. Who goes in must come out. You know the rules.'

The signs are up at the border. Anyone who breaks the rules has a death wish. Decapitated on the spot. A Pleasure Pass expires at sunset.

'Name your price...'

Greed lit up his piggy eyes. But his answer was still, 'Impossible.'

Was he bluffing? Trying to raise the stakes? I'm good at poker.

Da Cunta smelled his own fingers. A tell?

Has this snoop in his crummy suit, his face reeking of arrogance, his thick fingers stenching of yesterday: has he fucked my wife?

Did he go into the Pussy Parlour and rent her?

'I have kept my bargain. I found your wife. The thing that was your wife. We're done here.' Da Cunta laughed. 'Unless you can get someone to take her place.'

It was him who gave me the idea. Implanted it in my mind.

Da Cunta had reluctantly taken his leave, regretting the lost fortune. He couldn't get his stinky sausage fingers on it. Transporting live flesh over the border would cost him his life.

Why did she go to Fleshworld?

At least she is not infected. The flesh girls are tested. Can't be infected yet if working in a Pussy Parlour. But is she working? Or just in the window to attract business?

Get someone to take her place.

How could I even think of stealing this child and swapping her for my wife? I'll get us all killed.

Did I feel sorry for her already? The sad girl in the pink dress who has no control over her life. The worthless child who sits on the bar stool waiting to be violated. Ashamed of myself and my evil plan?

Premeditated sin carries the worst punishment. Damned forever. Barred from paradise. If you believe that sort of thing.

Evil, no matter how good the motive, comes to a bad end. There must be another way? An escape route that does not involve human sacrifice. A way of rescuing my wife without damning someone else. Does Ice even want to be saved?

She loves Fleshworld. Man after man filling her hole.

I am not even sure now if it is Mother's voice or mine speaking these thoughts.

I have to get out of here before I do something stupid. But this could be my last chance to save Ice, my only chance.

You don't want that cheap slut back. She's dirty now.

Out of the corner of my eye, I saw the pimp approaching.

He's young. Barely out of school, with that boyish swagger; foolishly fearing nothing. He reminds me of someone.

Before he had a chance to barter her, I upped and left, slamming the door behind me.

I'm driving but I don't know where I'm going.

Erasing everything from my mind except my wife: how she looked, standing in the window of the Pussy Parlour dressed as a flesh girl; the picture was burning a hole in my thigh. Even in that plastic pink mini dress with her naturals showing, she looks expensive.

How did Ice get stuck in Fleshworld? She must have had a pass to get in. Why didn't she come out? Did she get trapped there when the border closed? But why did she go there? The same questions, over and over.

It was not pity for the girl that made me hesitate. It was fear. Who will make *Safe* if something happens to me? The formula is in my head. We're all doomed without *Safe*.

You're so fucking weak.

Mother is right. I am weak. Making excuses. Afraid of failure. Scared Ice does not want me to find her. Scared she does not love me.

I don't care what happens to me if Ice doesn't love me. But I care about her.

If I don't act now, she will be infected. She has three *Safe* days left. I cannot allow pity for a soiled child to stop me.

The poor die young. Only the rich can afford *Safe*. The girl will be dead before she's 13 whether I ruin her or not.

Ice is alive. She was alive when da Cunta took her picture. I have to save her. Time is running out. Ice's time. I turned around and went back to the bar.

Making sure the pimp saw me order, I went outside and stood in the dark, waiting.

I can't be seen with the girl before she disappears. Let her follow me outside. The pimp will assume I'm shy. He'll send her out to me. A takeaway, to consume with my plastic cup of angel juice.

Trash

D*ry your eyes, and turn your head away...*

The haunting voice of the singer follows the girl out of the bar, reminding me of Ice. Everything reminds me of her. The cold moon staring over this twisted city; the stars lost forever behind Pure World's pain.

'What's your name?' the child asked, panting.

Air hissing out of her mouth, the lips thinner than they should be but her green eyes, incredibly, are the same colour as Ice's. The green of emeralds not envy, that Ice hides behind silver lenses.

'Richard,' I said, smelling her.

'What perfume is that?'

'It's just me.'

The girl is not bad looking in a white trash weekend way, but not like Ice. Not really. Same height and weight. Similar bone structure. Totally different essence.

Manky cunt.

But the expression on her face, hard to read in the

dark, reminds me for a moment of my wife. I can fix the hair and clothes. But is there enough of a resemblance for my crazy plan to work? Can I get away with making a switch? Confronted by her smile in the cold moonlight, it seems ridiculous. The plot of a madman, doomed to fail.

'Rich,' the girl said, annoying me. 'My favourite name.' She leaned into me, the way she has been taught by her pimp, allowing me to sense her naturals beneath their plastic coating.

'Richard,' I corrected her. My wife calls me Rich. Or she used to, when she was in a playful mood.

'What would you like to call me?'

'What's your name?'

'It's...what's your favourite name?'

She made as if to follow me into the car. I stopped her with my arm, aware I was hurting her as I pressed against her body. She didn't complain.

'You want to do it here?'

'Do what?'

'Bad will kill me if I go back with nothing.'

She stood there shivering in the cold, making me responsible. She's right. He'll make her suffer. These days I can't bear the thought of anyone suffering.

'You could go home,' I said, knowing she doesn't have one; making sure there's no one waiting to report her missing. Home is where the heart isn't. Why can't I switch off my memory, at least for tonight?

'My name's Trish,' she said, smiling like a broken doll. 'Trish White.'

For a moment I thought she said Trash Night. And

from now on, that's her name. Making her cheap and unreal, an object to be disposed of. That's what I tell myself.

We tell ourselves stories in order to live. The narrative changes. Or sometimes it remains the same. The same story over and over. The same search for salvation. All my life I've been looking for Ice.

Maybe she doesn't want to be saved?

I'll save her anyway. She's my happy ending. I can't leave her in Fleshworld to be corrupted by sex decay. There's still time to stop the ticking time bomb that will implode my happiness in three days.

I have to get Ice back. I need to make her safe. She is pale. I am dark. I am hers. She is mine. We belong together.

I open the car door, allow Trash to climb in, a babyish smile on her small face as she cosies up to me in the front seat.

I can smell her as her thigh confronts mine.

In this light, she is almost beautiful. I know what I am about to do, and I hate my cruelty. But that will not stop me. I have to get my wife back. This girl is not important. Her life is worthless anyway.

How could it be wrong to swap her for Ice?

Damn your evil soul.

It made me feel safe, knowing I was at the forefront of Mother's curses. Knowing she was scared to pick up the scissors; scared to be sent back to the House of Despair.

Mother is not here now. Just me and Trash disappearing into the night.

Driving too fast, aware there is no turning back once on the road to damnation, listening to Trash sing along to an old song, one that Ice liked.

There's nothing left to say...

There I go again, using the past tense. Ice isn't lost yet.

Suddenly Trash stopped singing, covering her mouth with her hand.

'Holy Luck, is that your house?!'

Trash gazed over the black lake at the bubble, her excitement increasing as the lights came on. She giggled when Rob saluted us as we climbed into the boat to sail across to my glass house. Showing off for her, I changed the colour to pink, making the child squeal with joy.

She held on to my hand after I helped her out of the boat. The bubble opened, allowed us to enter, then closed, encasing us, making us safe. For tonight. No one can get in, no one can leave.

I took her straight to the bedroom. She expected this.

For a moment I considered fucking her first. Why not, I've paid for it?

She must have sex decay. Not many younglings are contaminated; but her poverty cancels out her youth.

Disgusted with myself, I told her, 'Wait here. Don't

touch anything.'

I went into Ice's dressing room, aware that the girl was sitting on my bed holding her breath; a reflection of her skinny legs visible in the mirror.

Ice's clothes are arranged by colour. The Traviata-blue collection, the crimson rail, the blacks and creams that suit her skin. Frivolous yellow she never wore but it looks cheerful hanging there. Deep emerald velvet opposite the fresh greens of summer silk. I'm addicted to buying her things.

I selected a suit, sober yet sexy, which reminds me of the one the doomed blonde wears in the old movie *Vertigo*. Something made before even Mother was born, preserved in homage to the perfect past.

While she was getting ready, I went out on to the deck, smoked a cigarette; something I haven't done for years. My lungs tight with fear, I became aware of another sound, something that wasn't my heart.

The tracker is active! Ice has put her earrings back on. She's close! She's here...I ran inside, following the heartbeat of hope.

Trash was sitting in front of the mirror when I shoved open the bathroom door; a new expression on her tawdry child's face.

'Take them off.'

She starts to undress.

'Take those earrings off.'

'I was just...'

'Where did you get those?'

'I found them.'

'Where?'

'Here in the sparkly box.'

'You're lying.'

'I swear mister...'

I threw the tracker at the mirror, smashing it. Slamming the door, I stood listening to her sob uncontrollably. Does breaking down like that make you feel better? I don't know. I don't cry.

Trash came out of the bathroom wearing my wife's grey suit.

Seeing her flesh touching Ice's clothes disturbs me. But I have to see how she looks in them. Can I pull this off?

'Do I really look like her, mister?' she asks, holding her breath. I have spun her a story about my dead wife, how she reminds me of her. The girl cried as I told her.

The sight of her standing there in Ice's outfit excites me. Wrong, yet right. Not Ice, yet somehow, in the silk shirt and expensive tailoring, my eyes ignoring the girl's yellow hair…maybe we can pull it off? *We?*

Surprising myself and her, I slap her hard across the cheek. Her face crumples. Immediately I regret my outburst. I throw my arms around her and let her cry.

Holding her is strangely comforting, listening to her breathe. She is grateful for my arms, my handkerchief, the sudden calm. Sorry about the wet stain she's making on my beautiful shirt. Trash is the girl who is always sorry.

When she's finished crying, she looks up at me expecting sex.

Ignoring the coy pout, I take her to Ice's bathroom and wash her face. With her harsh make-up erased she looks even younger. And somehow more like Ice.

I run a bath. The bathtub full of blood is on my mind again.

Suppressing the image, I order Trash to get into the hot water. There will be no catastrophe in the bathtub. Once in a lifetime is enough for any man.

'With the suit on?' she asks, dumb.

'Get undressed first.' I manage not to sigh. 'I'll wait outside.'

'You don't have to do that Mr Richard,' she says, annoying me again.

I waited outside the bathroom door; my heart beating too fast. Why did Ice go to Fleshworld?

The manky cunt abandoned you.

When she didn't come home that day - was it really just four days ago? - Fleshworld was the last place I expected her to be found.

In my soul, I'd known all along. Though I don't know where knowledge comes from. These odd instincts inside us that confirm the truth or lead us astray.

Is anything true? Is everything an illusion? Like the landscape digitally created outside our window, the sounds in the room, the scent in the air. I have to give up introspection or I am lost. I must focus on my plan.

'Dry yourself then put this on.'

Without looking at Trash, I held out a white bathrobe; a new one, not one my wife has worn.

I caught a glimpse of her small naturals in the mirror as she dried herself. She is almost as white as Ice. The stirrings of my scarred organ annoyed me. I must control this reaction she arouses in me.

A distracted man can't accomplish a plan.

There must be another way?

Suppress that doubt. Kill it off. This is my plan. The best plan I have. The only one. This is what I must do.

Swap her life for the sake of my wife. Say it again into myself. Whisper out loud in the dark, like one of Mother's mantras chanted with her cronies in the Pure Party.

Sacrifice her life…for my Ice.

Do you want to go to Fleshworld?

Trash enters my room. Tiptoes towards my bed, holding her breath. I stay still, feigning sleep.

Has the girl come to kill me? She'd be trapped inside the bubble forever with me dead. No one to release her. She wouldn't mind. She'd have the time of her life. And, lying in the dark with this weight on my heart, how I long for oblivion. But if I die who will rescue Ice?

She will stay forever in that Pussy Parlour, pawed by sex tourists, fucked until her insides are scarred. Forever. Or until her beauty is contaminated.

Trash was almost upon me, creeping in on the bed, a timid spider. Suddenly I jumped up. She screamed, darted back.

'I'm sorry, Mr Richard. I had a dream…' She stood with one leg crossed over the other, sleep in her wet eyes.

'Stop crying,' I barked, pulling the sheet back in invitation anyway.

She climbed in beside me, staying on her own side.

On Ice's side. If she'd slept beside me. We loved in this bed, but she preferred to sleep alone, stretched out on silk sheets. Sex is easy, intimacy impossible.

I ran my fingers through the girl's frizzy yellow hair, imagining how it will look softened to an expensive blonde. She snuggled up to me, a sleepy kitten. It was not unpleasant having her in my bed. And while we're safe in the bubble, my wife is being violated by strangers.

I heard my voice whisper seductively in the darkness, 'Would you like to go to Fleshworld?' The question is alive with possibilities; an offer from Satan.

'With you? Like a date?' I don't answer. 'Yes,' she says, breathless and excited. 'Ooh, yes.'

Eager to please, to damn herself.

'This is a dream come true. I've always wanted to go on a day trip.'

A day that will last a lifetime.

Now that it is agreed, finally I am able to sleep.

Now that my plan is past the point of no return, my conscience, my fears, my memories of everything lost and broken in my life can take a night off. Whether my actions are doomed to success or failure, it is now out of my hands. All I have to do is follow through. And that's better than fretting. I am a man of action after all. Someone who gets on with it, gets things done. The man who gets what he wants.

That night I dreamt I was sailing amongst fjords in a pure, clean country where nothing bad happens. A little boring maybe, but a calm and restful place to sleep.

At my side, a woman smiles. I cannot see her face but know it is my wife. A chink of doubt in the dream implies this slender creature is perhaps my sister. The one my mother would have preferred to grow inside her instead of me.

I feel strange. The dream is telling me what I already know. I put it there, inside my head. Why deny it?

Doubt dissolves in the mist of this Shangri-la. Clouds float above and below me. Suspended in air, a sensation somewhere between erotic and soothing envelopes my senses.

And then Trash woke me up, spoiled everything.

Three Days Left

I listened to her clatter around the bathroom. She came out wearing the plastic dress from last night.

'Where do you think you're going?'

'Sorry Mr Richard, did I wake you? I have to go home and change.' Her face crumpled under my scrutiny. 'Are we still going on our day trip?'

'Yes, of course. But…take that hideous dress off. We'll go shopping, get you some things, take you to the beauty parlour.'

Sleep yawned out of me. I wanted to go back to that dream.

'Aaah!' she squealed out her excitement at the prospect of shopping. 'Can I call my mother?'

'Your mother?' Girls like her are not supposed to have a mother.

'She'll be worried about me.' Adding shyly, 'I ain't never been out all night before.'

'Call her later,' I said smoothly. 'We have to get moving.'

I hate the sound of my own voice. That doesn't

stop me talking.

In the jeep I asked, 'Does your mother know about your...work?'

Trash reddened. 'Bad isn't really a pimp, you know. Just a boy from my class in school. He was top in probability last year. Real smart kid. He can predict anything about anyone. Everybody likes him.'

This is getting worse. Next thing she'll be confiding that she's really 13 like Bad claimed in the bar. I'll be done for child abduction, paedophilia, and probably murder when she doesn't come home again.

'Before you, I only had one client. And that was just a wank jobbie. Messy but quick. A boy who beat Bad at poker. Must have been cheating. Bad always wins.'

'I'm not a client,' I said, panic in my normally calm voice.

'Of course not,' she agreed. 'You're the man of my dreams.'

And dreams turn so quickly into nightmares.

First stop the beauty parlour for a Transformation session.

'It's my daughter's birthday,' I'd explained to the beautician on the telephone. 'And she wants to look like a movie star.'

I sourced images of Hitchcock's ice blondes, my eyes lingering on the treacherous tramp in *Vertigo*.

‘I don’t care how much it costs.’

I drove Trash to the salon but waited outside, careful not to be caught on the snoopers. Hat pulled low, mask high, already covering my tracks, avoiding evidence. Using that trick my mind pulls in these situations: pretending it’s for her own good, her reputation would be ruined if seen with an older man. She would look like a prostitute.

I hate myself for this need to fool myself. But if I think the truth out loud, I may not be able to go through with it. And that condemns my wife to Hell. I can’t choose this child over her. Morality is about getting your priorities straight.

I pray that Ice is kept in the window, where da Cunta photographed her, a beautiful advert to attract business.

Come inside the Pussy Parlour. Meet the woman of your desires.

Safe in the window until I rescue her, not pawed by paying customers who buy perversion for the day, then take the train back to Pure World in time for cocoa with the kids.

Pray to who?

Ice never wanted children. We had a picture of the perfect baby. She composed it on her computer, taking the eyes from this child, the nose from that. The end product was a serene little girl with the composure of an oriental, the skin pure snow.

‘What is her name?’ I asked.

‘She doesn’t have one,’ Ice said firmly.

Trash comes out, beaming.

I will not say I did not recognise her. She was still in her go-go boots and the sweatpants I made her wear instead of her pink plastic flesh girl uniform. She still has the same eager expression and bow-legged walk. But her hair is lovely, glistening in the sunlight, flattering the paleness of her skin. No longer a brassy doll; now a consumptive princess. A girl who may die young but be loved until she does.

'I love you so much, Mr Richard,' she squealed, admiring herself in the rear-view mirror of the jeep. 'I'll do anything you want.'

This offer embarrassed me. To cover my unease, I said gruffly, 'Stop calling me Mr Richard for a start.'

'What should I call you then?'

I started to say Richard, but maybe it would be better to use another name.

'Dick,' I heard myself say. 'Call me Dick.'

We drove to the Wishing Well, stopping to call her mother at a terminal. I can't let her use my cell, and hers has no credit. This piece of information fell into my lap, reassuring me that she can't text for help tomorrow when trapped in Fleshworld.

'Sorry,' she said, climbing back into the jeep. The sweatpants show off the cleft between her legs. 'I had to call her.'

'What did you tell her?'

'Stayed with my friend Jemma – rehearsing for the school play.'

'What if she calls Jemma's mother to check your story?'

'I don't have a friend called Jemma!' she squealed, pleased with herself. 'So she can't call her mother.' Lies come easy to younglings.

We drove in companionable silence. I suggested she put on some music. She didn't make a move.

'You know,' she said, looking sad, 'my sister disappeared. One day she just never came home. Dirty Patrol told us it happens all the time. No body, no trace.'

This disturbed me. Coincidence lacks credibility. While I was still absorbing this twist in the tale, she said suddenly, 'Can we drink Martinis in Fleshworld? Dead glamorous cocktails. Not like the drinks at Paradise Alley.'

'Of course,' I heard my voice say. 'Whatever you want.' She snuggled up to me, pressing her hand against mine. The intimacy of this repulsed me.

It gave me pleasure to watch her in the dress shop. Selecting suits and dresses she will never have time to wear, but I bought them anyway.

And shoes, and gloves, and underwear. 'Stuff a real lady wears,' she said, happy with her haul.

She couldn't keep her nose out of the retro shoes with their scarlet soles and stiletto heels.

'Real leather,' she said, sniffing them before sliding

her foot back in. Only to take it out again a moment later. 'Even the lining is real.'

Real. That struck me. Something real in a fake world. Is it that easy to be authentic? A pair of expensive shoes in a natural fabric, is that the price of reality here?

My irritating attention to detail intact, I couldn't help but notice a little mark on her foot. A tattoo of a flower, a lily, which almost concealed another tattoo underneath. The name of an old boyfriend? Too short. Then again, she's the kind of girl to have a boyfriend called Ned or Big or, of course, Bad. Is that it? Does the schoolboy pimp stamp his name on the soles of his whores?

She was delighted with the jewels glittering in display cases but refused to remove her locket, sticking her chin out in a manner that reminded me of Ice. Did Bad give her the locket? A cheap reward for her services? Trash was firm in her refusal when I offered her a better one.

'No,' she said, 'I never take this off.'

She was dying to go home and show off her new hair colour.

Her enthusiasm was touching. I was torn between keeping her with me until tomorrow, when we would go to Fleshworld on the first train, and not wanting to arouse the mother's suspicions. She may call the Dirties if her baby daughter stays out two nights in a row. And Bad saw us drive off into the night together.

I made her promise to tell no one about me. She swore she would meet me at the station next morning on time.

'Cross my heart and hope to die,' she said, earnest.

And why wouldn't she meet me? She's said often enough it will be the best day of her life.

'Wait a minute,' I said, before she disappeared into the subway. 'What about the clothes? What will you tell your mother?'

'School play,' she said. 'Have to pick one as my costume.'

Sounds lame to me, but she was pleased with her excuse. Can't she just hide them under the bed? What do I know about teenage girls and their ways.

Later, as I sat watching the digital sunset, the violet one that Ice liked best, it occurred to me that Trash may have played me.

Her lost sister could be a ruse invented to match my lost wife. Something for us to share, a lost loved one in common. Just because there is dirt behind her fingernails doesn't mean she can't be crafty. Just because she looks innocent doesn't mean she is.

And my wife, my perfect Ice, now has two days left to live. To live clean and pure and safe; the only life worth living.

I switched off the cameras and went into Ice's room and lay on her bed sobbing. The sheets on her bed barely smell of her anymore. Soon they will have lost her scent.

Two Days Left

Six am. Standing on the bridge. Tense. Watching for her.

I shouldn't have let her out of my sight. What was I thinking? Did part of me want to give her a chance to escape my evil net? Sympathy for her is betrayal of Ice. I need to stay in control. Weakness has no place in my plan.

Maybe she overslept? She promised not to be late. She *promised*. I vowed never to trust a woman again. She is not a woman. She is a child.

Is she not coming after all? Did her mother overhear her last night, boasting to a friend about her rich boyfriend, and lock her in? Are the Dirties on their way now?

No. She wouldn't rat on me. And she'd rather die than miss this trip. She loves me. She thinks she does.

She isn't late yet.

Maybe something happened at the clinic?

I couldn't risk being seen there with her. I could have injected her with Ice's formula. They are the same blood type. But protecting her with Ice's essence, something I can't share myself, was repugnant to me. I'm jealous even of that.

Sending Trash to be inoculated was a mistake. What good will the vaccine do her when she wakes up in Fleshworld with no way home? Maybe it would be kinder for her to be exposed immediately, to die faster.

I don't even know for sure she went to the clinic. She promised she would go. But she could have used the money to buy herself another present. A present for the mother who should be protecting her.

She could be infected already. Then the jab will kill her. But that takes four days. Four is the unlucky thirteen in Chairman Luck's system of Chinese roulette.

Four days is enough time for me to make the switch. If she doesn't show today, I will hunt her. *Force* her.

Bloated, sad faces with no idea how to recognise desire troop onto the platform, clutching their tickets to Fleshworld. Their mixed up emotions a comedy in the dawn, it doesn't occur to them to seek true love. Paying for sordid pleasure is a safer bet.

Or maybe I'm the deluded one. A man in love with his own wife is after all a comedy. A wife he didn't really know. Ice is the woman every man dreams up in his head. The invention doesn't need to be conscious.

And losing your wife? How ridiculous is that.

What right have I to sneer at the fornication of others? Maybe it's best to keep lust and love separate in two sides of what was once the same city. Who am I to think I know better than Luck?

She isn't late.

Feeling sick, I watch her approach from my vantage point on the bridge. She's wearing a white dress with a pair of flat school slippers, carrying a satchel. She looks like a little girl.

Her new blonde hair gleaming in the morning dew, she tilts her face up for a kiss when she sees me. I turn away, avoiding the gesture.

'I told you to wear the suit.'

'Sorry, Dick.' The silly name irritates me, but I say nothing. After all it was my idea. 'I have it with me. And the shoes. Didn't want my mother to see me in it.'

'Go and change. Hurry up or we'll miss the transit.'

That isn't possible. I have reserved. I just can't wait to get to Fleshworld. Can't waste another minute. Need to get this over with before my resolve dies.

My heart freezes as she appears through the haze that passes for air wearing the violent grey suit, her hair pinned up; the high heels improving her posture. Ice is an original. Yet this girl could, almost, be her.

'Can we go in the pink one?' Trash asks.

She delights in the sweety-pink pod, suspended high above the black hole; the decimated river that once flowed between two halves of a whole city, now a swamp of despair. The flesh-eating insects can be seen swarming in their pit below, but only if you look down.

Trash stares straight ahead, the childlike joy on her face at odds with her sophisticated attire. We could be on a fairground ride. Anyone for candyfloss?

As our pod descends into the tunnel, preparing to deliver us to Hell, Trash sings along to something stupid. Music on a loop to drown out the screams of the flesheaters mass suiciding on the roof of their pit. It was a stroke of genius to imprison them in glass. A warning of your fate, if Chairman Luck's rules are not obeyed. A reminder that life is not endless; buy your fun while you can.

Every time I come here it looks different. Fleshworld stays the same, it's me who changes. When I truly believe the darkness in me cannot further blacken, evil wells up in my soul to take me by surprise.

Trash leans against me as we go through the tunnel, fiddling with the locket that's always round her neck.

I hold my breath, aware of the packet of *Sleep* in my pocket. Would it be kinder to inject her with all of it when I make the swap? Ensure that she never wakes up. Isn't that better than being abandoned in a Pussy Parlour on the wrong side of the border? Knowing that her hero has betrayed her. Is death better than betrayal?

Evil cunt.

Filled with disgust, I fondle the packet of *Sleep* in my pocket. Can't stop touching it. Hiding there, waiting for the kill.

Weakness annoys me. She's worthless. A little slut. Having the time of her life at my expense. Doesn't care about me; out for what she can get. Anyone's for a new dress and an ice-cream sundae.

What will her mother do when her baby doesn't come home? The memory of coming back to the bubble to find Ice gone is still raw. But Trash's mother is not my problem. Her life is not my life. Stop torturing myself with doubt.

I can't think about their pain. I must get Ice back before she is damaged forever. Before everything is spoiled with no dreams worth buying.

What kind of a mother is Mrs Trash anyway? A mother who doesn't ask questions. I had a mother who demanded too much. My incarceration for her murder was Mummy's love letter from Hell. The final blow that almost stopped me.

There is a theory that men marry their mother. That trap didn't catch me. Ice is not my mother. She isn't anyone's mother.

You are entering Fleshworld.

We came out of the tunnel into the neon lights sparkling in perpetuity.

Trash squeals, 'This is great!'

It does have a tarnished grandeur. A rush of heat overwhelms us. Peeling off my coat, I wipe the sweat off my brow; the way her cool hand used to when I was weary. Fingers adorned with diamonds, toes painted silver to match her fake eyes.

Trash removes her jacket, looks to me for approval, puts it back on. She must be sweltering. You can even smell the heat.

Cynics say it is hot here because Chairman Luck wants everybody naked. Realists say it's the price of burning all those lights night and day. Sometimes I think people come here for the change in the weather as much as the sex. Maybe that's why Ice visited?

No. That is not true. She enjoyed cold air, holding her face up to the rain. At least, I think she did. That was how it appeared to me at the time.

There is a problem up ahead. Someone in the queue is arguing with the guards. A round is fired, but no one falls. Warning shots.

Trash tugs my sleeve. 'Mr Rich…I mean Dick. Can I have an ice-cream?'

I give her a few coins. She gets a big cone with two chocolate spears sticking out of it and starts to lick. The heat is extreme, the ice-cream melts down her front. The queue isn't really moving. I strain to see what's going on.

She removes her jacket, sits on the ground, her face in the cone. She does not notice the flesh girl being decapitated and eaten by dogs. She was almost there, almost in the pod. Once its doors closed, she would have been transported to Pure World. But almost is not the same as escaping.

Trash is engrossed in her obscene cone. I cannot take my eyes off her. Biting the heads off the phallic flakes, her pink tongue licking the ice-cream with love; unaware of the dogs feasting on the dead flesh girl.

Ice will be with me on the transit back to Pure World tonight. And Trash will be left behind. Now I'm ready for the kill. Keen to be rid of her. I can't let her out of my sight until the deed is done.

Who cares what happens to her? Tonight my wife will be home, safe, in my arms. There is no cost too high for that.

But when did anything ever go as planned?

I'm Watching You

Ecstasy escapes from me as she lies on top of me, covering me, her smooth skin illuminated in the celluloid moonlight.

Her white shoulder blades betray nothing. The back of her head is unexpected, less familiar than her perfect face. You could burn her face with a cigarette and it wouldn't melt. I examine her eyes for traces of …what?

The contempt she conceals when she sees my mutilated naked body, feels the weight of its desire. No emotion is visible in this picture I have of her. Over and over, I watch the act of love between us on the screen.

Naked, sitting up in bed, worshipping Ice's image. I can hear Trash on the phone to her mother. I want to punch her hard in the face. Anything to make her shut up. She can't stop talking, she's so happy.

'Today was the best day of my life,' she says, as I lie on the satin bedspread, my wife's perfect nudity freeze-framed before me. It's all I have.

Quickly, I switch off the screen and cover myself as Trash comes into the room, face flushed with joy. The mother believes she's on a school trip.

'It's not really a lie,' Trash says, joining me in bed. Who asked her to lie down next to me in her white schoolgirl knickers? Probably soiled. Stained with something I don't want to know about. 'It was a trip and you sure are a friend.' She flushes. 'More than a friend.'

What kind of mother believes such nonsense?

The kind of mother who ignores the truth about her dirty daughter. Or a gullible woman, willing to believe in sudden good fortune: her clever baby has been chosen for a school treat. Like mother, like daughter; both the trusting kind.

I push her off the bed.

She whimpers, stands there on one leg looking at me, wondering what she's done wrong. At least she isn't apologising again, begging me to explain her flaws.

'Get out of my sight.'

'Where will I go?' she asks in a small voice. She thinks I'm putting her out. Banishing her into the cold night, dismissing her. If only.

'Take a bath.' Adding sadistically, 'You smell bad.'

I knew this would hurt her. I didn't expect the look of pure mortification she gave me. She touches under her armpit, sniffing her finger, before scurrying off to scrub herself.

Truth is she doesn't smell bad. She smells of Ice. She's been using her potions and perfumes. I want her to soak in Ice's scent, come out of the bath smelling even more like my wife. Distract me from my brain-damaging headache.

I feel like taking the packet of *Sleep* myself. But I will need it tomorrow. Tomorrow is my last chance.

The headache started this morning when we arrived in Fleshworld and were informed, 'Flesh Fair is closed today.'

The guard stroking his zapper ignored my protests and issued us with tickets for the Fun Bubble, where brats get taken on their birthdays.

Sheer frustration had me shouting, 'Do you know who I am?' The guard sniggered at my futile Mr Important act. Human and smug, he didn't even bother pointing his gun at me.

'Chairman Luck will hear about this,' I threatened.

'You better hope he doesn't.'

I could hear the dogs supping the last of the decapitated flesh girl. The one who almost escaped. Soon there will be no trace that she ever existed.

Trash tugged my sleeve. 'I've always wanted to go in the Fun Bubble,' she said, a stupid grin on her ice-cream smeared face. This is her fault. Licking obscenely in full view of everyone in the queue.

All day long I had to watch her eating candyfloss,

asking if I wanted a nibble.

She played hoopla with the other kids while my wife was within a machine gun sprint, a few streets away. Outside this diazepam funfair, Ice is breathing, swallowing, living without me.

Does she think about me? Dream of rescue? She must know I will come for her.

I used to feel her ignore me even while looking into my eyes. But things change. People change. Sometimes.

All day I suffered the agony of hope, wishing the Pussy Parlours would open. No one seemed to know why they were shut. A fat man in tartan shorts said, 'Even whores need a holiday.'

The funfair was full of strident laughter, a symptom of dismay, or relief, at dashed sexual hopes. No lust to prove, no charade of desire to perform. Everyone except me seemed to be enjoying the fair.

At sunset we travelled back in silence.

Trash looked scared. She knew better than to ask me again, 'Have I done something wrong?' But couldn't hide her disappointment when I hustled her on to the transit. No flying pink pod, gliding on its tightrope tonight; just a quick ride through the tunnel of Hell.

From time to time, I grabbed her hand, pulling her thumb out of her mouth.

As we sped through the black hole, the atmosphere changed. In an underground tunnel, it should be impossible to tell. But there's an eerie feeling of emptiness, magnified in everyone's eyes, when you are going through the pit. I glanced at the emergency door. Its red No Exit light was lit.

I checked my pocket for the packet of *Sleep* and discovered my phone vibrating. A message. The usual surge of hope came over me, still dumbly expecting news of Ice. We're in a tunnel. The message must be from someone on the train.

I locked myself in the decontamination room to read it. Tension gripped me before I opened the message envelope.

And there it was. In bold blue letters on the screen.

I'm watching you.

Splashing cold water on the back of my neck, I composed my features and returned to my seat.

Trash looked relieved. Could the message have been from her? She has no credit in her phone. She could have bought some. She could have been lying in the first place.

I searched her face. She looked up, hopeful of a small sign of affection. No, it wasn't her. Why would it be?

From behind my shades, I scanned the faces of those seated nearby. No one looked guilty. Probably younglings having a laugh. But how would they get my number?

I can't think about that now.

Once we were through the tunnel, on the other side of the black hole, I said, 'We'll come again tomorrow.'

Her eyes enlarged. 'Do you mean it?!'

Oh yes, I mean it.

She is still sobbing in the tub because I called her dirty. Little fool.

My phone rings. Holding my breath, I pick it up.

Nobody speaks. I can tell someone is there.

'Da Cunta, is that you?' Inside, I'm still hoping for a miracle. Maybe the crummy enforcer has got Ice back for me? The line goes dead. Hope is devious, endlessly teasing.

Who was it? No number listed. Wrong numbers are a thing of the past. It is someone who knows me. Ice?

Fear suddenly grips me, a violent suspicion has me running to the bathroom.

'You gave her my number? You told your mother my number.' I hold her head underwater. She's spluttering, unable to answer.

When I allow her up for air, her face is blue.

'No,' she says in a soft, scared voice. 'No I never.'

Somehow I believe her denial.

'I did promise Mother a present,' she says, sobbing again. 'I'm sorry. But I never told her your number or anything, I swear, Dick.'

I feel sick. Sick of myself, sick of her, and sick of

this mother's silent collusion with my evil plot. This mother who wants a present.

I dry her off and put her to bed.

'Can I sleep with you?' she asks.

'No,' I say firmly. 'Sleep here.'

I lie in the darkness watching the mini movie of me fucking my wife. I don't even know if Flesh Fair will be open tomorrow. Half of me hopes it will be shut again. If it is open, I will have to face Ice.

What if she refuses to come home with me? It will be impossible to drug Trash and make the switch without Ice's help. Why wouldn't she want to escape?

Wants to suck and fuck.

Doubt frightens me. My mind is crowded. At the heart of my misery is that question: *Why did she go to Fleshworld?*

Did someone force her? Was it blackmail? I know that is incredible. Ice was not the blackmail type.

There I go again, using the past tense.

But what if Mother is right. What if Ice *likes* Fleshworld. She was always so bored at home. Sighing at her beauty in the mirror, impatient for something to change, *waiting* for something.

Was I really surprised that day I came home and found the bubble empty? Or was the surprise just a sad promise: something inevitable I hoped to escape from anyway.

She does not love you.

I have examined her last day in the bubble a million times. No matter how long I stare at the screen, there is no trace of deception as Ice sits at her mirror, applying violet-tinged powder to her eyelids, staring the snooper in the eye.

Nobody loves you.

I locked myself in Ice's bathroom.

This room still retains her essence. The girl has been spraying her scent. Ice didn't need perfume. Her own smell was superior. But she was addicted to buying bottles of perfume. Most of the bottles are full. Did she use them? Replenish them frequently?

I know so little about her.

Sticking out of the bin, drawing my eye in. I see it. A clue? Left deliberately to throw me off the scent? To instil doubt? A pregnancy test, crushed; impossible to read the result.

Did Trash put it there? Or was it here all along?

Eventually I surprised myself by falling into a pleasant dream.

Ice is in the bathtub, her naked flesh tantalising under scented bubbles.

I move towards her, raw with desire. Climbing into the bath beside her, she smiles at me. I look at her, longing. And realise this naked woman is my mother.

I woke sweating to find Trash's soft, warm body pressed against my back.

That was the worst thing about the crone's last party trick. Worse than being locked up in that stinking cell, wondering if I'd ever be released, was the moment I saw my mother's naked body in the bath. The memory still makes me shudder. The sag of her naturals and the fear of white pubic hair lurking beneath the blood-tinted water.

That memory will accompany me beyond death. It disgusts me more even than what she did to me, though I live with the scars of that episode in our story.

But I'm lying again. Lying to myself. That was not the worst bit. What I did was the worst bit. Mother displayed her naked corpse, left it out for me to find. And I violated it.

I lay awake, listening to Trash's small snores.

Repulsed, I didn't move away. Ice would never force her flesh on me like this. But I don't want to wake her. I can't stand hearing her whimper again, not tonight.

Tomorrow is my last chance. Twenty-four hours left to save Ice before she's infected. I must find Ice and bring her home; or leave her behind forever.

I'm scared of failure. Am I also scared of success?

In the morning, Trash smiled at me before opening her eyes.

Her hand went first to her locket, checking it's still there, then reached out shyly to hold my hand.

Now that the deadline is closing in, I'm confident that my plan will succeed. I feel a pang of something I at first understood as regret but later realised is cruelty. Today I will make the switch.

Last Day
Inside the Pink Pussy

Trash clutches my hand, marking the flesh, as we enter the Pink Pussy.

A loud man ahead of us in the queue strokes his finger against the slithery pink surface of the entrance labia. After giving the finger a long suck, he pushes it into his companion's mouth. She giggles and pulls away, sweaty in the intense heat.

The Pink Pussy is made out of real skin. That's the rumour. It does smell real. But they could have got that smell anywhere. There's nothing that doesn't come bottled in Fleshworld.

'Bad's dream is to own one of these places,' Trash says, trying to act casual, hoping to please me with her passive acceptance of vice.

'And you working in it.'

'No!' Her face falls the way it does when slapped. 'I never would.'

A transi in a candyfloss wig with a punishment dildo strapped to her meaty thigh smiles at Trash, in kindness or invitation. Pink's the theme here, from the flesh girls' dresses to the currency collected.

Ice is not in the window today. In her place chained to a pole is a girl who looks even younger than Trash, legs splayed open to reveal her sex hole. Male fantasy is sordid but the Pink Pussy approves all tastes.

I'd dreaded seeing Ice humiliated in that pink plastic uniform. But if she was in the window, at least I could point and say, 'That one.'

But she's here. I know it. I *feel* it.

'Once inside the Pink Pussy,' the transi shouts into her megaphone, 'select what you desire. Kants and Kinks: all welcome.'

The queue was moving slowly, giving my eyes an opportunity to take in the layout of the Pussy Parlour. Inside there are two giant breasts: one for swingers, one for straights. How can anyone tell the difference?

I was dithering over which tit to enter when the transi poked us towards Kinks, winking at Trash.

'What if I don't find what I'm looking for?'

Ice could be in Kants. There is after all nothing kinky about her. She's a classic male fantasy. The one you can't own, even when you pay.

'Then come to Candy Dark, I'll help you uncover your fantasies.'

'I know exactly who I want.' I unclenched my fist, showing a handful of jewels brought as bribes.

'There is no substitute for what you really want,' Candy said. The hair regrowth on her hand as she grabbed the stones betrays her as human. The greedy way she pawed the rubies reminds me of Mother.

'Tell Candy, tell Candy all.'

'She was in the window last time I was here.'

A brief description sufficed. I didn't need to get out the photograph, half-mutilated in my pocket.

'Ice Queen.'

'Yes.'

'She is busy. We have younger flesh girls, more to your taste.'

'I just want to talk to her.'

'I bet you do.' Candy gave a stagey wink, poking us into the giant breast with her pink dildo.

Sweating under the throbbing light in our love cave, hope fraying my nerves, I'd almost forgotten Trash.

I became aware of her trembling; shaking with dread as two flesh girls closed in on us.

Trash whispered, 'They're joined together.'

Are they conjoined twins or a speciality act? Do they remove their costumes after work and separate? There is no after. Pleasure does not end in Fleshworld.

One half whipped me with the neon tail attached to their rear, while the other tugged at Trash's clothing, undressing her.

I picked up the dress, catching her scent as I folded it neatly into my backpack. Ice's dress. A vintage halterneck jade silk. One of her favourites. She wore it the day I bought her the blue diamonds.

'I adore diamonds. You can never tell what mood

they're in.'

'Diamonds are forever,' I replied, holding on to her. Expensive, brilliant, indestructible.

Trash started to cry.

'I want to go home.' And worse. 'I want my mummy.'

She clung to her cheap locket, afraid they would try to remove it along with her clothes.

'We have a shy one,' the twins said, continuing to peel off Trash's white bra and underpants. Nudity will make my job easier when I swap her with my wife.

As Trash sobbed, naked, in my arms, I asked the flesh twins to send in Candy Dark.

'Candy? Are you *sure*?'

I sprinkled sapphires on their torso. I've brought plenty of jewels. The twins grabbed them, greedy with delight.

'Tell Candy to hurry up.'

'Whatever turns your twist.'

Taking pity on Trash in spite of my resolve to remain detached, I wrapped a pink blanket round her. The synthetic fabric was uncomfortable against her skin, she had to shrug it off despite her shame at being naked.

The love cave's so hot it's incredible that it doesn't spontaneously combust. We were both sweating, a faint odour emanating from the folds between her legs.

'Can we go?' she whispered, holding onto the little ivory satin pouch with the mother-of-pearl clasp that I'd bought her against my better judgment. Not a lady's handbag. The sort of small treasure that goes in a child's coffin, filled with favourite things.

'Soon,' I promised. Adding calmly, 'Trust me.'

After some bargaining, Candy Dark agreed to take us to Ice.

'It's not jewels Candy needs, it's a way out of Fleshworld.'

I gave her a vial of *Safe*. 'You will test pure if you take this.'

Candy believes my lie. She wants to.

Sometimes I wonder if *Safe* works by auto-suggestion. You think you are safe. Therefore you are. Infection is all in the mind. I don't want to test my theory.

'They can't keep you if your blood is pure.' I told Candy Dark, improvising. 'You can just walk out the door. There must be a back way?'

'We specialise in back doors here.' I made a half-hearted smile at the lame joke. 'Can wiggle straight through the front door any time I feel like it. The exit chip at the border, that's the problem. Candy wants to keep her head.'

Poor deluded pervert. Candy wouldn't fit into Pure World at all.

'Cross with us,' I said smoothly, 'I have a spare chip.'

'Let's see.' Coarse laughter leaked out of me as the creature felt my sex parts.

'Later. Take me to Ice first. Ice Queen.'

'I don't believe you have a spare chip.' Candy stared hard at me. But she wants to believe. She wants to believe escape is possible.

'Is freedom worth gambling on?'

'Maybe not, but Candy will. What else does she have to do?'

As we followed the transi through labyrinthine corridors, Candy kept twisting round to say, 'I could lose my head for you.'

Trash held the little pouch in front of her sex hole, mortified by her nudity. Candy didn't bat a false eyelash. Naked flesh is her business.

The pink paint petered out and, after crossing a maintenance area with gigantic cylinders of chemicals, suddenly we were in a white, bright space.

I'm paying close attention, calculating the escape route. I have a good sense of direction and the compass in my pocket is displaying north-east. That means we are below the main entrance now. Not the best way out. Or, maybe... Back doors can attract more attention.

The Game of Luck

The sight of my wife overwhelms me.

My mind was occupied plotting our escape from this overheated dungeon. Suddenly she's before me. Ice, my beautiful Ice, perfect and serene draped in a pure white robe, the fabric flimsy to the point of transparency. She looks at me without recognition.

'Ice! Ice!' I reach out to her.

A glance betrays something then her face returns to neutral. She neither speaks nor makes any motion towards me.

Suddenly my hand thrashes against something cold and hard. I hit it again. Clink, like the sound of two ice cubes kissing.

My arm reaches out to the cold surface again. Candy grabs me.

'Careful, she bites.'

Ice is in a glass cage. Glass constructed to resemble the texture and reflective beauty of ice. Ice sits there unmoved, unblinking.

'What's wrong with her? Is she drugged?'

Candy points at the cerulean computer screen on the wall. 'That's her thoughts.'

The screen is blank.

Trash is pressing her face against the glass, mesmerised by Ice's beauty. Ice stares back at her, transfixed with her own reflection.

'Has she been brainwashed?'

Candy snorts. 'You wanted to see her. You have. Time for your part of the deal. Let's ding-dong.'

'Where's my chip for the transit out of Hell?' Candy demands, grabbing me by the throat.

Intelligence is the ability to improvise. I motion to Candy that I need a private word, and we step back into the corridor. She understands immediately.

'There is no spare pass? It's the child's pass?'

'Right,' I sound smooth and sneaky. 'All we have to do is get her in that cage.'

'Not possible. But I'll whack her over the head with this.' Candy swings her glossy dildo. 'Won't hurt a bit. Well, not much.'

'You have to open the cage first.' Candy looks suspicious. But she just has that sort of face. Paranoid eyes; tight, bitter mouth.

'I want to fuck the Ice Queen.' She finds this excuse plausible.

'Candy doesn't have the password to open the cage. Or I'd fuck her myself.'

'How do they feed her?'

'The Ice Queen doesn't eat much. When she wants something she opens the cage herself.'

Enjoying my surprise, Candy continues. 'Haven't

you heard of the game before? Luck's game? Everyone in Fleshworld knows it.'

'Well I'm from Pure World. Humour me.'

'Every now and then one of the flesh girls catches Luck's eye. So he puts her in here and reads her thoughts. The more he knows about her, the harder it is to escape. This cold bitch has barely blinked. She's definitely winning.'

'What's the point of the game?'

'What's the point of anything?'

'You said she's winning?'

'The flesh girls choose their own password, so only they can unlock the cage. But they don't. They die in it…most of them.'

Bingo. I know Ice's password. Something clear and pure to focus on, make her mind go blank. The survivor's best friend.

I ran back to the cage.

Ice and Trash were in the same position. Trash seemed to have fallen into the same hypnotic state as Ice. Or maybe she was just dazed. She looked absurd naked, clinging to her little purse. The sag in her naturals from slouching not catastrophic yet. They will be drooping to her knees by the time she's 30. There I go again, wasting time on irrelevancies. She will be dead before she's 20.

Trash whispered in a small voice, almost too quiet to hear, 'It's her.'

Ignoring her, I keyed *Safe* into the computer. The

cage didn't open. For a moment I was stuck, then it came to me. Second time lucky.

The ice cage opens. A flicker of irritation registers on Ice's face. I reach out for her. She draws back, angry. I can tell she's angry. No one else would be able to read her expression.

I pull her towards me. She resists. But I am stronger. I haul her out of the cage. And Candy ushers Trash inside.

'What's the password?' Candy asks. 'We need to seal it.'

I key Ice's password into the computer, while Candy restrains her. Ice sinks her teeth into the transi's cheek.

'The bitch bit me.'

It's no good. The password isn't working. I understand the problem. Ice's password is now invalid. Control is waiting for a new password from Trash.

Candy wipes blood from her face, whacking Ice with the dildo. Ice falls, dazed, to the floor. I seize the moment, sticking the needle of *Sleep* into the gash in the transi's cheek.

The big creature falls. For a minute I think I may have killed her. But no. *Sleep* gets to the brain faster when injected further up the body.

Trash is rooted to the spot. A look of dumb recognition mingled with comic book horror smothers her features. Emotions are mass market, picked up from old melodramas, derived in turn from Greek tragedy and God's daydreams.

She opens her mouth to speak. Her thoughts appear on the computer screen.

Rich Rich Rich don't leave me Rich.

Selecting her password, the ice cube clinks shut. Her fate is sealed. The last sight I have of her is the silent tears of abandonment that run down the screen.

There's a mark on my hand where she dug her nails in, holding it too tight in the queue to come into this vice palace. Maybe not. Her nails are short, ragged, bitten. The mark is more likely to be from Ice's fingernails. Oriental in their elegance. She specialises in drawing blood at first strike.

Ice allows me to remove the white robe and replace it with her own silk dress. Does she remember the feel of its fabric against her skin? It smells faintly of Trash, but still smells of Ice.

The candyfloss curls have fallen off Candy's head, revealing a scarred bald pate. Ice stares in fascination, ignoring me.

Ice's feet are bare apart from her signature silver toe paint. Walking barefoot across the red dust of Fleshworld will attract the wrong type of attention. Candy's gilt stilettos are far too big. But the vulgar shoes are better than the pink go-go boots the flesh girls wear. Those boots suit Trash but would look ridiculous on Ice and brand her as a flesh girl.

The clock's ticking. Candy could wake up any

minute. A silent alarm could have alerted the guards that the cage just opened. Luck himself may be on his way now.

I lashed my wife's feet into the big gold shoes and held her up as she tried to walk in them.

Goodbye to Fleshworld

We crossed the border safely, almost without incident.

Ice allowed me to drape my arm around her. As the guard inspected our exit chips, she flashed him a brilliant smile. As we were about to cross to the platform for the train back to Pure World and our old life together, a zapper went off up ahead.

'Somebody trying to escape?' Ice asked coolly.

The fat man in tartan I'd seen yesterday had fallen onto the track. Maybe not him, but another who looks identical.

'Pushing his luck.' The guard smiled pleasantly back at Ice. I noticed he hasn't collected her chip. She slipped it inside her dress. I envied it resting against her flesh.

We watched as the dogs devoured the fat man's corpse, splayed untidily on the track. Ice's eyes were feverish. I supported her slender body, wondering why she stole the pass? Does she want to return to Fleshworld?

I'm exaggerating. She didn't *steal* it. He neglected to take it from her, and, not having a pocket or handbag, she placed it for safekeeping on her person. The guard will probably collect it in a minute, once the excitement of the feast has passed.

But he didn't. He smiled at her again, waving us through to safety. Ice has that effect on men. They seek her approval. They want her to absolve the gravity of their sins. It's an emotion beyond sexual attraction; something inexplicable her beauty alone could not solicit. A power that she mysteriously possesses.

The work of the dogs was almost done as we boarded the train. A young man watched Ice from beneath the brim of his hat, his dark eyes hungry. I felt proud of my beautiful wife, happy to be close to her again. She was oblivious to his admiration. I should have been more alert, more watchful; suspicious of everyone.

Ice remained silent as we crossed the black hole, smiling at me when I caught her eye. We never used to talk much anyway. After a good night's sleep in her own bed, she will be completely herself again.

A storm was descending as we arrived in Pure World. A real storm, not the digital kind she likes me to produce. Her favourite weather is a good omen.

The low flying drones, adorned with ruby and emerald searchlights, circled reassuringly above the station; protecting us from intruders. Intruders are not always human. The air needs to be kept clear of plague, clean and cool like my wife's heart. There's a rumour that Luck has an invisible flypod that he uses to ride the skies.

Maybe I will never know why she went to Fleshworld. Needing the answer to everything is a weakness. Sometimes the question is best left unasked.

She thanked me as I enclosed her in the white fur wrap, unfurled from my backpack. We were like any other rich married couple returning home, faintly tired after a pleasure trip, as we waited for the Rob to bring our car round.

Nervous, I checked my phone. Nothing. No need to worry. No cryptic messages today. Everything is going to be all right. Everything is good already.

Deluded fool.

Shut up.

'Huh?'

'Nothing darling. I forgot to switch off my phone.'

The silver-blue light of the approaching storm illuminates her as she crosses the bridge, looking pleased to be home.

The giant trees guarding our bubble cast a shadow over her. Protective or threatening? Two sides of the coin of love.

Ice hurries inside as the bubble's door opens. The alarm sounds. The security system has auto-erased her, a safety net built into my cautious system. Trash's frequent presence has overridden the machine's memory of Ice.

Ice ignores the alarm, going straight to her bathroom, while I disable the alert. I can fix it later. For the moment, no one but me can enter without activating red alert. No one but me can leave. This is reassuring yet disturbing. Am I making her my prisoner? It is for her own good, until I find out why she ran away to Fleshworld.

She allows me to inject her with *Safe*. I've made the deadline with hours to spare. But I give her an extra shot anyway, to be on the safe side.

As she sings softly in her jasmine-scented bath, I collect the exit chip, discarded carelessly on the floor with her clothes, and conceal it in the sole of my boot.

'Fix me a drink, darling. A blue Martini.'

She is acting like nothing's happened. This is strange, yet convenient. I don't want to upset her raking over her captivity in Fleshworld, not tonight.

In my mind that's what it has become: imprisonment. The chains mental not physical. Something binding her to the Pink Pussy, thwarting her will to escape.

Is Luck a machine? Could a man really create a city as evil as Fleshworld?

He wants your wife. He'll take her back. He's coming.

I mix the drinks and take them upstairs.

If Ice was in a trance before, the spell is now broken. She seems to have forgotten everything. As her naked perfection rises from the fragrant bath-water, that question still nags at me.

Why did she go to Fleshworld?

I can't think about it now. I'll ask her tomorrow.

Why can't I be more like her? Why do I have to understand everything. To know everything. My wife is naked in my arms, I don't need to think. She is everything I want.

After being satisfied, I carry her to her bed.

I don't want to push my luck. Make her feel trapped. She prefers to sleep in her own bed.

She yawns, stretches, slips under the covers.

As I kiss her goodnight she whispers, 'In the morning, this will seem like a dream.'

Immediately I fell into a fevered sleep.

The beep of my phone woke me. I switched it to silent then checked the screen in the dark. Blank.

I tiptoed into Ice's room. Beauty is asleep wearing her blue diamond earrings; her face angelic.

Angel was her password. That's me, her guardian angel. Trash has chosen Rich as her password to open the ice cage. Or rather the computer – Luck? – has selected it as the key to her heart. Rich and rich. Me and money: conveniently the same thing.

Don't think about Trash. Trash is nothing. A nobody.

My phone vibrates.

Leaving Ice sleeping peacefully, breathing like a sweet baby, I went into her bathroom and closed the door.

The blue text stares up at me:

HELP ME

Sweating, I switched off the phone.

It's from her. It must be from her. Surely she isn't waiting for me to save her? How stupid can she be.

Splashing cold water on my face, I sit on the edge of the bath. I switch the phone back on. Another message.

Please come back.

And a third.

PLEASE

Fuck. She's a wound that won't close, worrying the nerves, refusing to scab over.

I went downstairs to mix a Martini. Old-fashioned drinks are the best, a combined high of relaxation and glamour. Good for the body and the spirit.

The screen's on, showing the flesh flick I don't need to watch now. I have Ice back. For a moment, my attention is distracted. She's smaller from this camera angle. From behind she looks like Trash.

And then I notice him, slouched down in the chair smoking one of my cigars. Without embarrassment or effort at concealment, the intruder smiles and says, 'Mix me a drink, Rich.'

Bad

'How did you get in here?' I asked, sounding like a bad movie. Does anyone ever have a single original thought?

'Your wife let me in, Rich. Or should I call you Dick?'

I know that isn't true. No one but me can unlock the bubble. Ice is upstairs asleep, helpless. She cannot escape or issue invitations to intruders.

Anyway, the idea is preposterous. I know my wife. She could have Chairman Luck if she wanted. This lout who sells schoolgirls in a bar on the wrong side of the pleasure zone is not in her league.

But do I know her? Do I really know her at all? All I know is what she's told me. Why do I assume that others are telling the truth? I lie all the time. I never confess my secrets.

He could have sneaked in while I was resetting Rob. But Ice would have seen him come into the bubble? I make a mental note to check the snooper.

The boy watches me weigh up the situation,

wondering if I can jump him. He's younger, but I'm fit. He doesn't appear to be armed. He looks hard, but is he?

'Sit down, Dick. It's time for us to have our talk.'

'You know my wife?'

'I know that lady intimately.' He pauses, pleased with this word. 'She's my favourite pink pussy.'

I raise my arm to strike him but in my anger misjudge the blow. He pushes me over on my back, pinning me down on the sofa.

'This is cosy,' he says, hurting me. I can see myself reflected in his bad black eyes. From this position, I can't help but notice that he's wearing my shoes. Buckskin monogrammed moccasins with a soft leather sole that Ice bought me for my birthday. The kind of gift you give your father, if you have one.

'What do you want?'

Laughing, he releases his grip. 'You know what I want, Dick.'

'Money?'

'It's not that simple, dude.' He looks pleased with himself. 'Have you ever woke up in the morning and just felt like being somebody else?'

Does he know something? Or is he bluffing?

'Maybe just become that person, you know?' This sends him into grunts of laughter. He's drugged or drunk or both. But he knows.

'Who would you like to be?' I ask, stalling.

He doesn't stop me when I get up and go to the cocktail cabinet. If I can get some *Sleep* into his Martini, everything will be ok. A few sprinkles should do it. I have some stashed in the ice drawer.

'Let's see.' He accepts the drink from me, but doesn't sip. 'Maybe I could swap lives with you? We look alike, kinda. I'm younger of course. And much better looking. But same height, same colour hair. And I've had practice fucking your wife.'

'But what's in it for me? Why would I want your life?'

'How about I don't tell the Dirties you abducted a 13-year-old girl. That's the kind of shit that gets you fried.'

'I haven't killed anyone.' But he's right. It's the kind of crime you can't buy your way out of in Pure World. Except there is no crime without evidence.

'You were the last one to be seen with her alive.'

What evidence is there? I bought her those dresses, but I paid cash. Will they remember us in the shop? Expensive stores like that don't want bad publicity. They don't want to be known as the place that sick sugar daddies take their sluts.

Who saw the clothes? Her mother? She's hardly innocent herself. She should have taken better care of her baby girl.

Why did I buy those damn dresses? In the end she wore Ice's dress anyway. The suit from the first day had ice-cream on it, and the others she'd left at home under her bed. Fuck!

'The one who took her to Fleshworld and left her to die.'

'Who knows which one of us they'd believe. A bad boy who doesn't go to school or a respectable older gentleman like me.' I sound calm, convincing. 'An inventor who keeps the world safe.'

'They might believe what they saw with their own eyes. Like footage of you two walking hand in hand into the Pink Pussy.'

'And you think Luck would give a fuck about that? The man who allows children to be chained in Pussy Parlour windows?'

'He may pass it to the other side. Now he knows his favourite pussy isn't in her cage.'

Is that all he has? I sink back into the cushions, relieved. Pure World and Fleshworld are two separate zones. That fact is crucial to their survival. Illegal sins on one side are acceptable desires on the other. It's the secret of the success of our split city: one side repressed, the other possessed. This immoral order would be disturbed if Luck's men with their hungry dogs and libidinous sneers co-operated with our anally retentive Dirty Patrol.

And Luck, the more I think about him, probably doesn't exist. He's a communal fantasy figure; a hybrid of God and Satan. Someone men aspire to be but fear at the same time. Invented to watch us because we are too tired to watch ourselves.

'So what do you think, dude? You want to try being me?'

'I think you'd better get the fuck out of my house.'

'Ok, dude, if that's what you want.' He gulps back his drink. I watch him too intently. Nothing happens. 'But first I'd like to give you a little present.'

He hands me a photograph. Me and Trash in the

dress shop. My heart beats faster, a catch in my throat at the sight of her innocent face. But I have no time for regret. Pity is a luxury for the blessed.

'You two look good together,' he says. 'There isn't a bad picture in the bunch.'

My mind is racing, thinking ahead of me. 'What about her mother? Has she reported her missing yet?'

He laughs. 'She doesn't have a mother.'

'Everybody has a mother.'

'You could say I'm her mother.'

We both look up at the same time. Ice is descending the stairs, backlit by moonlight.

'Hello beautiful,' he says. 'Remember me?'

She smiles at Bad, doesn't look at me.

Leaning seductively over him, stopping my heart, she closes in for a kiss. Suddenly her left arm swings up and she hits him hard with something silver and heavy. He reels back, stupefied. And Ice slips the handcuffs around his wrist.

'Help me.'

We drag him to the air grille, attach the other handcuff to the shiny metal.

'Bitch,' he spits at her.

She removes her white silk pyjama bottoms and ties them round his throat as a gag. Tying it tight, expertly. As she kneels over him, I check to see if she is exposing herself.

'We have to kill him,' she says. 'A blackmailer always comes back.'

Bad kicks out, my moccasin flying off his foot. But Ice avoids the blow, and jabs him with a syringe of *Sleep*.

Ice Blonde Thaws

She sits opposite me in the dawn, drinking coffee from a white cup at our kitchen table. She looks lovely, face free of paint, her eyes their natural green.

'Just kidding,' she says. 'We don't really need to kill him.'

'That's a relief. It's hard burying a body when the ground is covered in frost.'

She laughs, then becomes serious. 'You must erase your crime. Then there is no crime.'

'I have to get Trash back?'

'Yes.'

'I have to save her.'

'Bring her home.'

Home? Trash has no home. Does she mean bring her here to the bubble? Or back to Pure World?

'How old is she?'

'He says she's 13,' I say, ashamed.

'How could you have left her…in that place?'

'I had to get you back.'

'It's...' She stops herself.

'Evil?'

She stares out at the sun rising over the lake looking sad.

Finally I ask the question. I have to ask, or it will always be there invisibly between us.

'Why did you go there?'

'You wouldn't believe me,' she half laughs.

'I might.'

'I'll tell you. I promise I'll tell you everything. But first we have to get that child back before Bad wakes up. We have to hurry.'

'I have to get her back. I'm the one who left her there.'

She sits on my bed watching me dress.

I can't go to Fleshworld until the transit opens. We're both waiting for the hour to strike, waiting for the barrier that's still between us to disappear.

Suddenly she says, 'I did a bad thing.'

'Just one.'

She smiles. 'I lied about my age.'

'You're really 124,' I say, buttoning my combat shirt, filling the pockets with jewels and cash: the best weapons in Fleshworld.

'I'm not the age I said I was.'

'You'll never look a day older than 25.'

My obsession with her beauty irritates her.

'I never told you about my past.'

I sit on the bed beside her, heart beating fast. Information is dangerous. It preys on your mind. Dreams are contagious. Good ones, bad ones. Viral, bacterial. I haven't told Ice about my mother. I told her she's dead, but not that she tried to frame me for her murder.

Is she about to tell me something that will spoil our dream? And why is she telling me now, when I need to focus on finding Trash. Why is it suddenly important to tell me?

I want to hear her story, but I'm scared. This is the moment I've longed for and dreaded: becoming close to my wife. Knowing her as I know myself.

'When we met I refused to fall in love with you.'

'I noticed.' She silences me.

'I didn't want to love again.' Dread seeps through me. She is in love with someone else? She went to Fleshworld to look for him?

'Did you go there to find someone?...Someone you love?'

There, I've said it out loud. My fear contaminates the air between us, keeping us apart despite her proximity on the bed.

'Yes,' she admits. 'But stop asking questions. This is hard.' She takes my hand in hers. My hand is warm, hers is cold. We are compatible.

'I refused to fall in love with you. I trained myself not to. But...' She shrugs. 'I loved you anyway.' I took her in my arms. She pulled away. 'I have to tell you. I have to finish it. I may never be able to say it if

I don't say it now.'

And she told me the terrible thing she did, before she met me.

We've been married for ten years and I never had a clue. She had erased every trace from body and mind. Every outward trace. That's how she survived the ice cage in Fleshworld: she had perfected the talent of making her mind go blank, thinking about nothing. Because thoughts are painful.

Ice abandoned her baby sister. Her parents died, leaving her small sister in her care. She tried to love her, but couldn't. She hated being poor, being burdened. Being responsible for this tiny thing, having an obligation to love it more than herself. A baby that interrupted her own childhood. A baby she found it hard to look at.

'I left her on the steps of the House of Abandon. I can't see her face anymore in my imagination but I can still see her little fat legs running up the steps. She waved goodbye to me, standing on the steps, smiling. Two years old and two feet tall. Her smile hurt most. Her certainty that I was coming back in a little while to finish the game.'

Ice met me and her life became safe. She didn't have to worry anymore about getting ahead, getting rich. She was rich already, living out her fantasy as the perfect wife.

Without worries, she had time to think. She started to think about the baby. She considered confessing to me. She was about to tell me the night I suggested we go to the flesh party, which seemed to be the catalyst for this nightmare.

She accepted this party as her punishment for being a bad person, a deceitful wife, a traitor. She pretended punishment was pleasure.

Next day she visited the House of Abandon, feigning interest in adoption. There she discovered her sister was gone. She had run away, probably across the border for life as a flesh girl. Being adored by queues of men seems glamorous to an orphan; learning the dark arts of desire in Luck's pleasure state.

'They see the twinkling lights across the black hole,' Matron Correction explained, 'and crawl like maggots into a pit of vice.'

Ice looks me defiantly in the eye. She says, 'I could make myself noble and say I went to Fleshworld to look for her. But really I knew she was already lost forever. I went to punish myself, to suffer what must have been her fate. And…I don't know why…to punish you. To make you sorry for taking me to that sordid party. To make you sorry for loving me.'

A tear runs down her cheek. 'I was afraid to show you my fear and desire. In case you would stop loving me. And I hated you for that.'

She stopped, expecting me to respond. I couldn't speak. A weight had lifted from me. For so long I had suspected she was in love with another man. And all this time, he was me.

'And I know now that murder is better than

abandonment. The stain she left on my soul made it impossible to love without pain. So. There it is. My sad story.'

This time when I took her in my arms, she didn't resist.

Afterwards I held her close to me, whispering, 'We'll find her.'

My soothing voice reminds me of my invitation to Trash, that night in the dark, in this bed.

Would you like to go to Fleshworld with me?

Ice shakes her head. 'I've looked everywhere.'

'All those shopping trips when you bought nothing?'

'Yes.'

Shopping for a new soul.

'I promise we'll find her.'

'Don't make promises you can't keep.'

'We won't stop looking until we find her.'

'It's too late. She could be anywhere.'

'I found you.'

'How would you know her? She won't have the little fat legs anymore. At least I hope not, for her sake.' She laughs. 'Beauty is a curse women can't survive without.'

'There must be a way. I won't stop until I get her back.'

She stops me from making impossible promises.

'Find this other child. Return her to her mother.'

Clean the stain from our soul.

After kissing her goodbye, and warning her again to make sure the sleeping beast doesn't wake up, the last words she said to me were, 'I'm scared.'

'I'm scared too, but I'll be home tonight. Nothing can take me away from you.'

Nothing would make me leave her with Bad except the necessity of righting this wrong, redeeming myself in her eyes.

'After this, we will never be separated again.'

It was a promise I intended to keep. But promises are made to be broken.

The Other

Early morning darkness feels different from late-night dark. Somehow it is possible to tell the difference, even when locked in a dungeon.

My prison is not Ice's white, bright cage with the password to freedom on the wall. An old-fashioned lock and key secures my captivity in this hole with a shitter in the corner and an infested bed on the dirt floor. It could be that other cell they locked me in when Mother's corpse pointed the finger at me.

Is that it? Am I back in the Dirty House, arrested for murdering my mother? Was the rest of it all a dream? I didn't invent *Safe*, marry Ice and, almost, live happily ever after in a bubble floating on a lake.

When I open my eyes, I see Candy Dark watching through the bars.

'Good morning,' she says.

I have no idea which morning. I know enough not to ask Candy outright.

'Nice to see you again.'

'You'll be seeing a lot more of me.'

What's that supposed to mean? Surely rape is not possible? Chairman Luck neuters Pussy Parlour staff to prevent them from wearing out the sex slaves.

'Stealing my shoes,' Candy says, an expression of pain on her painted face. 'That was low. A woman loses her authority without her shoes.'

She is not my enemy or my friend. Just trying to save her own soul. This thought chimes in, unbidden. Empathy is a slippery slope. What next? I'll feel obligated to forgive my mother?

'I'm sorry about what happened before.' I felt in my pocket for my stash. 'But I came back for you...I can get you out of Fleshworld. If you just let me out of this hole.'

Candy pulls something out of her knickers. 'This what you're looking for, traitor?' Brings new meaning to the term 'filthy money'. I laugh in spite of my predicament.

'You won't be laughing when Chairman Luck is finished with you.' Candy Dark has something else in her hand. My eyes are gummed up. I'm having trouble focusing.

'I am sorry, really. I had to take my wife home.' A choice between saving Ice or keeping a promise is not a choice for me.

'I've been calling your bitch wife,' Candy says. 'Never home. You sure you can trust her?'

And with that parting shot Candy flounces off. The click, click of her departing heels confirms she has acquired a new pair of vintage stilettos.

I sank back onto the bed, thought better of it, stood up. Already my body is a mass of bites and welts. None of them festering yet. That means I've been here a week tops. Maybe just three or four days.

How can Ice be out? She's locked in. Secured inside the bubble by my aura. I remembered before I boarded the transit that she couldn't get out, but I was in a rush, and, I told myself, I'll be home tonight.

But I'm not home. And my wife is locked in the bubble with Bad. Has he got free from the cuffs and hurt her?

She let him in.

He was wearing my shoes. Rob mistook him for me. My feet must stink.

How did he get the shoes, stupid.

Trash gave them to him. That's it. It must have been Trash. She's the one conspiring against me.

Trash wouldn't do that. She loves you.

Gnawing doubt, never far away, comes at me as I pace the cage. Did Ice know Bad before? Why did she gag him?

To shut him up.

He's the boy I saw her flirting with in the bar?

They are in it together.

In what?

Fucking.

Ice loves me.

You are impossible to love.

She is perfect. I am a marked man. My scar has started to hurt again. Maybe it never stopped. Maybe I just got used to the feeling.

In our ten years together, I was careful never to let Ice see me fully naked; concealing Mother's messy attempt to transform my sex organs from boy to girl.

The mark is hidden, but still there; a part of me forever.

Ice loves me now. But soon she will start to hate me.

She can't bear excrement. It's been days now, maybe a week. Bad is bound to have taken a shit. He's the kind who would do it out of spite, right there on the white carpet.

Ice will hold her nose and run for the exit. And discover I've accidentally left her locked in. But was it an accident? Is that true? Or did part of me deliberately leave Rob programmed for my aura only? Despite our new start, did a deep, sad part of me still not trust her to be there when I got back?

An inability to accept good fortune, a refusal to believe in resurrection, is a major disability. Has Mother crippled me for life?

Trapped in the bubble with that poisonous smell, Ice will blame me. After all, it is my fault.

There's enough food and water to last for a long time. But if I die here, Ice will die too; trapped forever in our glass bubble with Bad and his shit.

How am I going to get out of here? Candy Dark has my bribes already. What am I going to do?

On the short train ride from Pure World, that day we parted – yesterday, the day before? - I had been distracted. This horrible mess could have been avoided if only we had trusted each other.

It's my fault. I never shared my secrets. If I sensed that she had something concealed behind her silver eyes, sad memories she could not allow me to witness; she must know that I do too. I must tell her everything as soon as I get back. If I get back.

I'd pretended that Mother was over and done with. Best forgotten. But I carry her evil revenge inside me. A legacy of hatred and deceit. And the burden of denial, pretending I don't care that I was mutilated by my own mother. Her love was worthless anyway.

I was right and I was wrong. Walking away from pain into the future is a good path. But it is hard to follow without looking back. Pus trapped below the surface of the skin turns into a boil, like the insect bites on my back. I'm refusing to scratch. But still I feel them itching.

I wasted energy mistrusting my wife when I should have been loving her. Telling Ice about my mother could not erase the nightmare, but it would have proved that I trusted her.

You sure you want to tell her about us?

Shut up.

I won't tell if you don't.

Alarm bells rang as soon as I stepped through the gate into the pleasure zone. The guard pointed his zapper at me, poised to kill. A voice behind me said, 'The Chairman wants him alive.'

They were expecting me. The stolen chip I'd brought for Trash must have alerted the system. As I fell to the ground under blows to the back of my head, I could hear the bark of hungry dogs and the sound of a child singing 'Favourite Things':

Of course I want platinum and diamond rings
A girl must have her favourite things

Mother interrupts, standing over me with no underpants on.

Just you and me now.

You are not here.

Who are you talking to then?

Shut up.

What will your wife do when she finds out?

She'll never find out.

Murdered your own mother.

You killed yourself.

Did I?

I was found not guilty.

You were sentenced to death. Bought your way out.

Ice will forgive me. I'll tell her what you did to me.

She'll never forgive you for Trash.

How did you get in here?

I'm always here.

She stretches her legs open wider.

What do you want?

I know what you want.

Mother lifts her dress revealing the black hole of flying flesheaters. But it is Candy Dark standing over me, flanked by two henchmen.

'Time to get lucky.'

And the syringe of *Sleep* slides into my arm.

The Mutilation of Mother

I am standing alone in a bare room.

How did I get here?

There is no door. No windows. No join in the walls where a door may once have been.

Rubbing sleep from my eyes, I examine the space again. Am I dead? Is this Hell? Trapped in a blank eternity, separated from Ice.

Suddenly I realise I am not alone. He is standing right in front of me. How could I have missed him?

'You broke the rules.'

'Who are you?'

'You know who I am.'

'Luck?'

His face comes into focus. His face is my face.

'Chairman Luck.'

Do I have a twin? The lucky boy who escaped Mother's scissors?

'But...'

'I am you.'

I reach out to touch his face, check that he is real.

There is a barrier between us.

'It's a mirror.'

'Clever Dick.'

'You take the features of the person you are talking to?'

'I look the way you imagine me.'

What did Ice see when she looked at you? I don't ask out loud, but he knows what I am thinking.

'She saw what she wants most.'

She didn't see you.

'Her self?'

'She saw her child.'

'She doesn't have a child.'

'You believe that?'

'What do you want?'

'I want to play a game.' My face cracks into a smile. 'Since you're so clever, we could call it a test. Pass the test and go free. Fail and die.'

The wall opens. Ice and Trash are chained to a pole. Trash is crying, but Ice is unmoved. She stares straight ahead, not seeing me. How did he get her out of the bubble?

'Rich,' Trash cries. 'I knew you'd come.'

Ice says nothing. I try to catch her eye but she has the same blank stare as before. She must have switched off her mind again so that Luck can't use her thoughts against her.

'Once you have selected, you can leave with your choice.'

'What about the other one?'

'What do you care?'

She will die a slow, disgusting death in the black hole.

'Yes,' Luck says, in answer to my thoughts. 'The flesheaters will feed on her.'

Is it him talking, or me?

He is you. Evil cunt.

'Flesheaters don't devour quickly like dogs, they have patience to savour their food. Thousands of them sharing one flesh, attracted by blood, seeking the warmth of a beating heart. Given enough time to feast, they grind up the bones after consuming the organs. I don't care for spectator sport myself, but it is popular.'

Trash is wailing, begging me. Her neediness is repulsive. But who wouldn't be terrified? Ice's calm is unnatural, even for her.

Suddenly I understand the fascination men feel for Ice. Luck wants her to want him. Her power is her indifference. She must have driven him mad, ignoring his will while in the ice cage. When I look at Luck, I see myself.

She has a child? Is that true?

Who's the Daddy?

Her body is unmarked by childbirth.

One of the men who's been up her hole.

Can't think about that. Can't *care.* Focus on making her safe. *Safe* is my business. How I made my fortune. How I won her love. *Safe* buys health. *Safe* buys beauty. The cold hard indestructible beauty of the blue diamonds in her ears. The power of…

'You have one minute to choose between them.'

Luck adds a flourish of showmanship, upturning an old-fashioned egg timer; its black sand diminishing time.

The power of... Of course. That's it. I know the answer.

'Make your choice,' Luck warns, 'or lose both forever.'

I know what I must do, but still it makes me balk. My hand points at Trash.

'Trash,' I hear my voice say. 'I want to save Trash.'

Trash runs to me, throws her arms around my neck, kisses me. Captivity in Fleshworld has aged her. She doesn't look like a child any more.

'Thank you, Rich.'

'I wasn't really picking you.'

'I saw you.'

'That is not my wife. It's a picture.'

'But how will your wife feel about being betrayed in favour of that?' Trash stands in her pink plastic flesh girl uniform, crossing and uncrossing her legs.

Her cunt is itching.

Shut up.

Did I say that aloud? No. I don't think so.

Candy materialises in the room, full of her own importance.

Luck orders, 'Take her back to work.'

'You promised we could leave,' Trash says in a small, bold voice.

'Ah, promises…' Luck sighs dreamily. 'Have you never broken a promise, Dick? Have you kept a promise?'

He winks at me, his mouth forming into an obscene pout.

The picture of Ice disappears from the wall. The pole her image had been chained to melts. Is that my last sight of my wife?

'Since you long to save Trash,' Luck says pleasantly, 'you can take her place in the black hole as supper for the flesheaters. We'll sell tickets.'

As he spoke, Luck transformed into my mother. His voice remained mine. But my death warrant was sealed against the backdrop of Mother's unpleasant laugh as Candy Dark returned Trash to the Pussy Parlour.

What sort of person am I?

Worse than me.

Abducting a child and stranding her in this cesspit. Could Ice forgive that?

That's not the worst thing you did.

Shut up, Mother.

I'll tell her.

You are not here. Shut up.

She'll be disgusted with you.

I can't hear you.

You know what you did.

Is that the real reason I left Ice locked in the bubble? Am I afraid that if she finds out, she will leave me? Worse, she will stop loving me.

She told me to make it right. To get Trash back. And I have failed.

Trapped here in this dungeon of despair, I am only now realising the enormity of my betrayal of Trash. I may as well have raped and killed her myself. That would have been better than sentencing her to this. And pity has only come now that I face death.

You've done worse than that. To your own mother.

Ice may never trust me again. But I must tell her everything. Every sickening detail, even that most repugnant act. That thing I can't even say into myself. The act that soiled my soul. I don't deserve Ice if I keep on lying to her. Concealment is just a passive form of lying.

What do I mean *tell her*?

There will be no opportunity to tell her. This time there is no reprieve. My fate is sealed. In less than an hour I will be eaten by a plague of flesheaters. Satan Graham is not coming to bribe fate this time.

Luck has not given a time for my execution, preferring to leave me in the limbo of uncertainty. But I know it will start before the Pleasure Passes expire. A showman could not miss an opportunity like that. Providing a tantalising glimpse of terror just before the sextrippers return over the border to Pure World.

During the day Fleshworld belongs to us, but at night the flesheaters rule. Massive ticket sales are assured to view the feed on my flesh. Will the flesh girls gloat at my doom, savour the sight of me being devoured? Or will they pity me?

Luck must have a few party tricks up his sleeve to make this a night to remember. You have to agree, he's a genius. A mad, mythical genius, who understands desire and punishment.

And can I claim that I do not deserve to die? Can I beg for mercy? Is God listening?

Only Mother, sitting inside my head with her sewing, having the last laugh. She will not desert me. I should have turned away. Left her in the bath of blood. Forgotten her.

I was home free. She was dead. Drowned in her own blood. I ran down the stairs two at a time like on that other night when she tried to unman me with her scissors. But I went back up.

The hole between her legs watches as I stick my tube inside her.

Go on. Fuck me. You know you want to.

My greatest invention was in my head already. I had the formula. I needed the ingredients. And then I had opportunity.

Evil fighting evil, that was my excuse, as I violated her corpse. Her open hole leered at me as I harvested her secretions. That indestructible gene, able to reinvent and protect itself, would complete my formula.

Was harvesting her essence a sin that cannot be erased? Without her I would not have been able to manufacture *Safe*. That is what made me. Using the filth that was my mother, I came up with an antidote.

But each time I inject myself she enters my bloodstream. Spreading her venom into my soul, toxic and invincible. Her essence of evil and fortitude, used to control the replication of plague.

Plague cannot be contained. It mutates faster than

sin. Soon nobody will be safe. And I will die with this stain on my soul.

Saying the words aloud, telling Ice what I have done, how I have sinned, would that absolve me? Would Ice go on loving me if she finds out I used my mother's secretions to make *Safe*?

I will never know.

The Black Hole

The smell of burning brings me out of my dark daydream.

Are they stoking a fire to burn my remains? No, the flesheaters will pick me clean. They are in for a treat tonight. Perhaps a bonfire to keep the crowd warm as they salivate over my death? Unlikely, given the intense heat of Fleshworld.

The fire must be a figment of my imagination. The end of me, burnt at the stake, an old-fashioned vision of Hell.

My phone vibrates. A new message. I know without looking it is from Mother.

I'm coming for you.

Why did I come back here?

Why didn't I just kill Bad and stay at home with my wife?

Was I looking, after all, for an excuse to fail at

happiness? Was I afraid to try and live with both her and hope?

Ice sent you away.

She sent me back to undo the evil I had done.

She wants him.

I wanted to erase my crime, to remove evidence it had occurred, return my victim to her old life. Erasure is different from atonement. One tidies up the loose ends, the other washes away the sin.

Men rarely have time for courage. I am practical, not noble. Goodness is something I have not mastered. And now I am out of time; alone in the dark waiting for death.

Still fumbling for excuses, still showing off for Ice, trying to make her admire me. Leaving her a memory to love: her husband died trying to save a child. A ruined child who cannot be saved, only taken back.

Still, I want to control everything. Not just myself but her too. Her feelings and thoughts. Even death and what happens after, I want to own that.

Chairman Luck is the same as me: selfish and shallow. Yet I lack his ruthless gift for cruelty. Cruelty for its own sake repels me, reminding me too much of Mother.

I am not brave. I am a man who loves his wife and wants to go home and hold her in my arms. Instead I am going to die. I wish I had never come here.

The smell of burning flesh overwhelms me. There is no clean air in Fleshworld. Down here in the dungeon, toxic fumes intensify. I want to die. I want to get it over with. What's left of my life can only be torment.

My wish is granted. Suddenly the key turns in the lock. It is time. The hour of feasting is here.

My lenses are struggling to adjust to engulfing blackness. I hold my breath, awaiting the rough touch of the guards, listening for Candy's taunt. Instead a small voice whispers, 'Rich?'

Don't answer. It's a trick.

But next time she speaks, I am certain it is her.

'Everything's burning,' Trash says, unlocking my cage. Still she is clutching the ivory purse I gave her, singed and pathetic, and wearing that gold locket around her neck.

'Did Luck send you?'

She looks puzzled. 'Of course not. I stole the key from Candy Dark. Everybody's running from the fire.'

'What fire?'

'Something exploded. I came straight down here to find you.'

'I'm sorry,' I say, meaning it. 'For leaving you here.'

'It's ok,' she says, reddening. 'I did something bad too. Something terrible.'

'We have to get out of here.'

'I stole your shoes.'

'It doesn't matter.'

'I gave Bad your shoes. I didn't want to steal from you but he kept on at me. He really wanted your shoes. And…he was my only friend. Before you. Didn't seem fair for me to suddenly have so many nice things and him to have nothing. I gave him all the money. But he wanted your shoes, the ones you had worn on your feet. He…'

'It doesn't matter. We have to get out of here. Now.'

'I'm scared. Let's stay here and die together.'

'I will keep you safe.' I almost told her to trust me. But I can't say that out loud. Not again.

'It's dark.'

'I can still see.'

'You can see in the dark?'

'Night sights.'

'I swear to God that's all I took. The shoes.'

I took her hand in mine, dragging her along the smoky corridors.

No resistance, no locked doors. The system must have been tripped by the fire. Either that or Luck is playing an elaborate hoax on everybody. Paranoia is hard to shake once the habit is formed.

Outside, the city is ablaze.

Flesh girls and sextrippers are running in every direction. Scarlet flames eat up the synthetic sex zone, making it impossible to tell which way is home.

Staring at the setting sun, I attempted to assess the direction of the border. But the sun is fake like everything else in this half-remembered dream, it follows Luck's rules.

A transit pod hovers on a wire above, its electric flight stopped abruptly when the system went down.

'It's our pod,' Trash says. 'The pink one.'

Her sentimental joy at seeing the pink pod that brought us here on our fleshtrip almost breaks me. I am to blame for everything. I have suspected for some time. Now I know for sure. I'm destroying what I built, burning my shame.

But if I am Luck then I know the way out. He always leaves himself an escape route.

And then I saw the magnificent flight of flesh-eaters flying to freedom. Will they transform into snow bugs at the border, blending with the scenery in Pure World? Or die of cold? Who knows what will happen next. Now they are dark stars leading us to safety.

'Come on,' I pull Trash towards the flames.

'Where are we going?' She looks uncertain, but she trusts me. Still, after everything.

'I'm taking you home to your mother.'

She reddens. 'I have no mother. I always wanted a mother. So I made one up.'

'It doesn't matter.'

'It was all lies.'

'Everybody lies.'

I spray us both with a pump, advertised as love juice, most likely fizzy water with a sticky thickener added in the mix. 'Don't be afraid of the fire,' I tell her. 'Just keep hold of my hand and we'll walk through it.'

'But Rich...we'll burn.'

'No. The fire isn't real. Do you trust me? It's fake. The fire can't burn us if we don't believe it will.'

I sound more confident than I feel. She takes my

hand, even managing a smile.

Her hair is burning.

I pull the flesh girl wig free, throwing it at the swamp. Too late to save Trash's baby fine hair, but in time to stop her scalp burning. Instinctively, she touches her hand against her newly bald head.

'Almost there,' I say, encouragingly. Even though we still have to cross the black hole. The flames now behind us, we are about to step into the pit of Hell.

Trash looks uncertainly at the black earth, hesitates. A woman with worms slithering into her ear pushes ahead of us. Burning bodies jump into the swamp. I thought I saw Candy Dark thrusting forward; her desire to escape stronger than fear.

Sex lepers are crawling on their hands and knees over the black hole. They lack hope. They don't believe they can make it to the other side. The girl's sad eyes follow them as they sink into suffocation.

'Come on, I'll carry you.' Still, she hesitates.

'It does matter.'

'What?'

'Not having a mother. A home.'

'I know.'

She allows me to hold her. I help her climb onto my back and we begin the dirty journey through the black hole. Its glass roof has shattered. The flying flesh-eaters are halfway to freedom on the other side already. They believe that it is possible.

Trash is heavier than she looks. I'm tired. The

smell of rot disturbs my senses. I want to drop her, press ahead alone, home to Ice.

But I can't, I have to save her. If I leave her here, in this rotting graveyard, I will never be clean.

Just keep going a little longer, haul my burden through chaos, then I will see Ice again. Home, safe. Now I am glad that I locked her in the bubble.

Locked in with Bad.

Nobody is listening to you.

In your shoes.

I'm busy.

Thanks to Trash. Scheming little slut.

The flying flesheaters guide us across. As we get closer to Pure World, they bind together to survive the cold. Adaptable, the way species that inspire disgust need to be. Their finely tuned survival instincts protect them from a world which recoils from them. The black mosaics look almost human, flying through the burnt sunset.

We emerged from the black hole to find the border guards have fled and filth is flooding the clean side of the city, two halves once again becoming one.

I set Trash down on a wall, pausing to rest. It is useless trying to find my jeep. An explosion, probably from the heat, has destroyed the row of buildings closest to the border on this side of the hole. Trash stares, transfixed.

'Can you manage to walk now?' She nods. 'What's wrong?'

'That,' she says in a small voice, staring at the rubble. 'It's the House of Abandon. Where they take babies nobody wants…I used to live there.'

I follow her eyes to a freshly erupted piece of waste ground. 'I'm sure they got the children out in time.'

'They ink a number on your foot in case your mother comes back for you. I waited and waited. Then Bad rescued me.'

'When was that?'

'Just before my birthday. I wanted to leave after, in case they baked me a cake. But Bad couldn't hang around for birthday cake. He says girls are past their best by ...'

'Come on, we have to hurry.'

'Where are we going?'

'Home.'

I don't want to take her home with me, spoil my reunion with my wife. But what can I do? I'd be burning in Fleshworld if she hadn't unlocked my cage. She did more than that. She made me see my self.

It isn't much further. Soon, I will be home with Ice. My wife will know what to do with this broken, bald, motherless child.

But when we reached the bubble, sweating and dirty, my home was empty. Ice was gone. Bad was gone.

There was no sign they had been confined here except the handcuffs chained to the grille, dangling on the clean white carpet. And his picture of me and Trash discarded on the white rug.

'Bad sure looks like you,' Trash says, picking up the photograph. 'Think he cut his hair that way deliberate. On account of his great admiration for you.'

I grabbed the print from her hand. She flinched, expecting a blow. She's right. It is not me in the picture, it's him. My guilt fooled me. The evidence against me was a hoax. Relief followed by rage. I have just been through Hell for nothing. But the question on my lips, the one that will remain unspoken, is this.

Was Ice in on it?

Did she send me back to Fleshworld to get me out of the way? Who is Ice? Did I make her up inside my head? A perfect wife to compensate me for my imperfect mother?

The bitch played you.

Swallowed my soul whole then spat it out for fun. She's gone, gone, gone. Leaving me with the trash.

She doesn't love you. Nobody loves you. Nobody will ever love you. You are evil. Impossible to love. Luck didn't control Fleshworld. It was you.

Mother is right. I am Luck. But I'm not feeling lucky now.

The Red Apple

I ran from room to room calling her name, knowing I would not find her. She's gone. Lost forever, like the child she loved.

Out of reach but always in my heart; the shadow on my soul which disappears at the sight of her will now darken and deepen.

When I went downstairs, my tears finally dry, Trash was kneeling before Ice's portrait, worshipping her beauty like she did that day when she stared at her in the ice cage. That day feels like forever away, that day of false hope.

Trash has kicked off her Pink Pussy go-go boots. Her feet must have been killing her hobbling here in those heels. The soles of her feet are branded with the pink plastic, its dye staining her white skin. She will leave footprints on the carpet.

Looking at her feet, suddenly I understand. It was staring me in the eye. Avoiding the obvious is a delaying tactic, inevitably having to look at what I don't want to see.

Did Bad know when he asked her to steal my shoes that would gain him admission to the bubble? Personal odours cling longest to the feet.

Or did he desire a pair of soft leather shoes and the rest was chance? The opportunity arose for him to run inside when Ice's return set off the alarm?

No, he planned it. He wanted my shoes, the girl said so, even though she gave him all the money. He could have bought his own.

It does not matter now. I no longer care to make sense of it. Life is full of unanswered questions which distract us from important truths.

I can see the mark of the House of Abandon, tattooed on Trash's foot, covered by the little flower of her choosing. She has tried to turn something ugly into something beautiful; transformed the stain of rejection branded on her at birth into a lily.

And suddenly it dawns on me, the thought I have been refusing. This dirty doll is nobody's daydream; an obscenity of need as she gazes at the picture of Ice. That does not mean she does not belong to someone.

I sprang on her from behind, shaking her hard. 'Have you seen my wife before?' I am shaking her so hard she cannot answer.

'I saw her in Fleshworld,' she says, catching her breath. 'And here. I saw her picture here.' She nods at the one on the wall.

'Before that?' I insist. 'Had you seen her?'

She hesitates, afraid of angering me again.

'I...she looks like my mother. How I imagine my mother. I don't really remember what she looks like, not anymore. I wanted to be beautiful…like her.'

'How old were you when you went to the House of Abandon?'

'I don't know,' she says, tearful. 'I swear I don't remember.' She fiddles with the cheap locket miraculously still attached to her throat.

Suddenly I felt pity for her, ashamed of my rough treatment.

What fantasy am I concocting now? I have lost Ice, but I have her child? Is life really that neat? Do lost children ever find their way home?

It is not her fault. None of this is her fault, she just happens to be here. She has nowhere else to go.

I put her to bed in Ice's room. After I've tucked her in and turned out the light, she whispers into the darkness, 'Do I look ugly with no hair.'

'No. Not ugly.' Adding with a smile, 'A little bit funny looking. But it will grow. Go to sleep.'

Will it grow? Will anything ever grow here again?

Standing in the dark, I stared out of my bubble, like I did that night I lost her, listening for her footsteps tapping across the iron bridge.

The snow is melting on the lake, every new star in the sky lit with the reflection of orange and lilac flames. Beauty means nothing without her. Beauty is Ice.

And she's out there, lost, somewhere in the dark

where I can't find her. Why didn't we escape to Utopia? Why did I leave her alone with Bad?

I have to get her back. But I can't. She has to want to come home. I know that now.

Exhausted, I lay down on my bed.

It feels like centuries ago when I sat here with Ice, hearing her story, her face clean and her eyes restored to their natural green. I looked at the clock.

20th June

Was it really only yesterday I left? Is that possible?

I switched on my laptop. It really is 20th June. One day forward. Time, like everything else, feels different in Fleshworld. Captive time is slower than pleasure time.

I clicked on the news. The city is in chaos. Everyone in the House of Abandon and the Dirty House killed in the explosion. At least those stupid Dirties have been erased.

And the children, I wonder, are they worse off dead? Maybe some of them grow up whole, but most of them are warped forever. How could it be otherwise? Trashed by their own mothers.

Of course having a mother did not stop me being branded.

I lay back down on my bed, hopeless. The smooth sheen of the sheet didn't soothe me. I sniffed the pillow, hoping for Ice's scent.

And then I saw it. The flesh-pink envelope waiting for me on the pillow. How could I have missed it? My hands trembled as I tore open the thick paper.

Darling,

I didn't tell the truth yesterday. Not the whole truth, as my father would have demanded. 'Tell the whole truth, Lily my girl,' he used to say, pointing his finger at my heart.

Is memory ever reliable? Of course it is. Though sometimes memory and imagination are the same. How we imagine ourselves is how we become.

That's why I'm afraid. Afraid of you knowing the evil secret that is my past. Erased long ago from my memory. But it found me again. I have always known it would. It was dangerous to fall in love. Love made me feel safe, lowered my defences against that old nightmare.

After you left I was happy, telling myself you would make it all right, come back to me and make me safe again. Until I remembered you still don't know everything. You haven't read my story. How could you have missed it? I thought when you came home and found me gone my diary was the first place you'd look.

Maybe you wanted to miss it. To keep me as your own perfect Ice? Secrets are only secret until they are spoken. Confession changes everything.

A part of me doesn't want to find my child, to discover what she has become. What I, in my neglect, have made her. Because absence is another form of evil.

But I must find her. I must go on looking. Or what I have lost will always cancel what I have gained.

That boy Bad couldn't resist showing off to me. He boasted how he got in here, so I knew how to get out. It is always possible to escape. Captivity is a state of mind.

He knows the runaways, lost girls with nowhere to go

except the arms of a bad man. They have no choice. And sometimes that seems easier, sacrificing your life to the will of another. But I am a grown woman with choices, not a child any more trapped in the dark.

I have gone with Bad to the House of Abandon. I can't wait for you.

It's strange. A part of me is sure I will never see you again and a part of me is certain that I will.

Who knows if you will want me once you know the truth? But please don't hate me. Imagine me as I was before, clean and hopeful, before I had committed a betrayal that makes me, forever, unworthy of love.

Your Ice

Heart thudding, I read the letter again.

What does she mean, unworthy of love? Always, the entire time I've known her, I've suspected something. I thought it was my own sordid past creeping between us, the tainted blood I carry in my veins.

I'm being ridiculous. How bad can her secret be? Another man? What does that matter, if she loves me now. She's alive, I can feel it. She will find her way home.

But what if she doesn't? What if I never see her again? Is it best to remember her the way she looked yesterday when we said goodbye, her green eyes clear and shining with love?

My diary was the first place you'd look...

Her diary? Ice doesn't have a diary. I have snooped through all her stuff. Where could she have hidden her diary?

My hands shake as I click on the blue screen, bringing her computer to life.

I see the file straight away. How could I have missed it? The title stares me out, mocking me.

Confession changes everything.

In a second, I could delete this confession. Empty the trash box, remove all trace from the hard drive. But her secret would still exist. It would still be eating away at me even if I do not know what it is.

Fretting over possibilities is worse than the truth.

The truth is never as bad as its author imagines. That's what I thought, before I read Ice's story. I truly believed that it couldn't be that bad.

My vision of Ice is inviolable, incapable of altering. I was convinced that nothing could corrupt my idea of her.

How innocent I was then. How foolish. How wrong I was.

The green apple of temptation, the red apple of damnation. Or maybe it's the other way around? My colour scheme could be unreliable. Memories are in black and white.

My hand reached up and plucked the crimson apple from the tree.

Part Two

Ice's Story

'I tried to drown my sorrows, but the bastards learned to swim.'

Frida Kahlo

You have to get close to smell someone.

The smell is what punished me afterwards. Suddenly on a train I would come too close to an armpit and imagine, for a moment, that it was him. But he would not travel by train.

This was before the city separated, before the air of Pure World became cold. There were still smells in the street, children playing in patches of sunlight. I walked to school alone, taking the same route each morning. I was ashamed of my parents and our shabby home. I had invented a mansion with servants, and couldn't risk any of the other children finding out the truth.

My parents were Purists in the early days of the party, when no one believed they would triumph. They were not cruel, just simple people who thought the division of the city would solve everything. Decadence on one side, decency on the other.

Even before I ruined everything, taking away their respectability, they constantly reminded me, 'You don't want to waste yourself, Lily.'

No, I didn't want to waste myself. I had plans, big plans. Already aware of my power, I was planning to use my beauty to leave my dull life behind. I couldn't wait to grow up. The beginning of our lives are spent willing the age clock onwards, until suddenly we want the clock to stop.

The car followed me for three days before he spoke to me.

I called it the liquorice waggon, it was long and black and shiny. I was in the habit of spitting out liquorice if I tasted it unexpectedly in a sweet. I should have known. But he beckoned and, defying my parents, I climbed into his car, smelling the leather seats.

He wanted to be sure, he told me afterwards, once we were safe inside his big house with the door locked. He sat me on his lap and said, 'I wanted to be sure you were the one, my one true love.'

He was fatter than I'd imagined my Prince Charming, but self-possessed. His confidence and the cigar smoke and the low murmur of his voice were seductive.

I couldn't call it rape, what happened in the fat man's house. I did not know the word. I was 13 but had never heard of sex. My parents had been careful. I had heard whispers at school, but closed my ears. I didn't want to waste myself.

It was painful what he did to me, it must have been. But I couldn't really feel it. My limbs have always been flexible. And my mind, my talent for blanking out, helped me erase most of the pain. But still I remember the smell, the smell of his sweating flesh. I worried I may throw up all over his damask bedspread. I worried I may die before the end.

It was something I had to do, a ritual to be suffered to initiate me into a different life. A life of things I couldn't even imagine. Safe from the taste of boiled cabbage, the touch of rough sheets scratching my soft skin, the eyes of my parents always on me.

After playing this game he told me I could never go home again. My parents would say I was dirty and send me away. I may as well stay with him.

This did not trouble me at first. I sensed that his threat was a lie. He would not tell my parents what he had done to me, and they would never guess. I could go home any time I felt like it.

I was curious about his house, its many rooms. It reminded me of movies my grandmother loved to watch about a place called Hollywood. Nice movies, no filth in any of them. But when she died the Purists destroyed her screen anyway, just in case demons lurked in its innards.

The fat man fell asleep, giving me an opportunity to have a snoop.

There was a pink room full of toys, baby things. He must have a wife and baby who are away somewhere.

Another room was covered with photographs; horrible pictures on its walls. I didn't want to look. The other rooms were musty, almost empty, the curtains closed in each one. It was time to leave.

The front door was locked. I couldn't find the key. With mounting panic, I searched for a window to crawl through. Each of them in turn mocked me as

I pulled back the thick velvet curtains to reveal bars. Even upstairs, the windows were barred.

I tried the telephone. The line was dead.

The fat man's house was well back from the road in secluded grounds. No one would hear me scream.

There were stairs leading down to the cellar, stairs that smelled of death. I wondered if there could be a way out down there hiding in the dark. I was afraid to go down those stairs, but I had exhausted all other possibilities of escape.

After checking that he was still asleep, I tiptoed down the stairs, holding my breath. It was obvious when I was halfway down that this was no way out. The cellar was black and airless.

I turned to go back up but before I reached the top, the key turned in the lock.

I lay in the dark, forgetting to breathe.

The dancing of raindrops almost soothed me to sleep. At ceiling level, there was a small window. I imagined I could see the sky. But the window was steamed up with condensation, revealing nothing but mist.

Piling up the junk in the cellar until it made a precarious ladder, I climbed as high as I could then stretched my left arm up; leaving my imprint on the window pane.

I fell down and climbed up again, pressing my fingertips on the glass, making my mark. When the rain stopped the condensation evaporated and my fingerprints disappeared.

I heard the fat man's footsteps on the stairs. This time I knew what was going to happen.

The next time, it hurt even more.

But I was always relieved when he took me out of the cellar. I would have done anything to be let out. I closed off my mind and lay still, waiting for it to finish.

He turned me over and I started to cry. The smell was suffocating even though my face was smothered into the pillow. I wanted to die. I begged him to let me go.

He told me to stop crying. It was not possible. I could not go home. And then, with a smile like he had just thought of it, he told me, 'Yes, there is something. A new game we can play together. After that it will be possible for you to go home.'

She was a beautiful child. I found out her name afterwards. Mimi. When she said it, pointing at herself, I thought she meant Me Me.

He waited in the car while I fetched her from behind the Chinese restaurant where he had seen her play. She was sitting on the ground, her fat little legs tucked up under her. She smiled straight away, delighted by me. Taking her hand, holding it tight, she came easily into the car.

Enjoying the adventure, Mimi ran gleefully up and

down at the fat man's house. He promised I could go once I helped bring her here. But locked the door as soon as we came in.

I pretended to play with the baby while watching him in the mirror. He put the key, carelessly, in the pocket of his trousers. Why hadn't I checked there that first night when there was still hope of not being soiled forever?

In my mind I believed it was possible to save Mimi as well as myself. I could run for help, bring the Dirty Patrol back in time to save her. She was so small. Surely he wasn't going to touch her? He must want her for some other reason. Perhaps to replace the baby that used to live in the nursery upstairs?

My days in the cellar had hardened me. I couldn't jeopardise my own escape worrying about her. So I pretended he was not going to hurt her when he took her into the nursery.

I sat listening on the stairs. I heard everything. This time there was no smell, I was not close enough. I heard her cries and his grunts as he rent her body in two.

I heard all of it.

And then the screams stopped. But still I heard them. I still hear them. The screams stopped. I'd wanted them to stop. They stopped. And that was worse.

Did you ever wonder why I needed to take *Sleep*?

During the day, I trained my mind to forget. But at night Mimi came back to haunt me. Death steals and memory returns, destroying rest with its demands.

I have long forgotten what he looked like, the fat man, all I have is his smell; disgusting me on the bodies of others. I could pass him in the street, or meet him in Fleshworld, without visual recognition. But his smell will be with me forever.

Your smell is something I love, the clean smell of goodness on your skin. Your scent lingering on your silk shirt is what first attracted me. Your silk shirt and your toned body beneath. No flab, no weakness. I noticed straight away, standing next to you in that elevator, ashamed of my cheap red dress.

You do not know how clean you are, how good. Concealing the poetry of your own soul, longing to be loved; unable to see that you are.

I stopped to collect myself.

How clean you are, how good.

Thought I heard Trash call out in her sleep. Ignoring her nightmare, I continued reading Ice's story.

The fat man came out of the nursery, naked, and went into his own bedroom. I don't think he saw me on the stairs, or heard the humiliating puddle of urine trickling down each step. He had forgotten me. His mind was elsewhere.

I didn't have much time. I knew I had to go

into that room and get the key from his big smelly trousers, discarded on the floor. I had to go into that room and get the key without looking at the baby.

It is not the baby anymore. The baby is in Heaven. Children go to Heaven when they die, even bad ones. Tears streamed down my cheeks but I made no sound as I went into the nursery. Silent tears are more painful.

My fingers recoiled from the fabric of his trousers as I retrieved the key. I tried to pull it out of his pocket without touching. I had to lean in close. His smell engulfed me. I could smell his sex tool. I could hear my own heartbeat accompanied by the drip of a single tear. But he didn't wake up. He lay snoring in the room next door.

I paused before I left the nursery. Maybe she's still breathing? Should I take her with me? At least try to save her. I wanted so much to save her.

I covered the baby with a pink blanket from the cot. If I hadn't caught sight of her face one last time perhaps I could have pretended she was sleeping. But no baby sleeps with a face like that.

My parents were afraid when they saw me. I had been missing for three days. They knew immediately that I had wasted myself. I told them about the fat man but left out the part about the baby. I couldn't bear to remember that out loud.

My mother scrubbed me clean in the bathtub, disinfecting the scalding water first before sliding me in. Afterwards, without looking at me, Father explained that I must never speak of these things. No one must know the White family's shame. I nodded agreement.

My father called the Dirty Patrol and explained in a voice phoney with joviality that they had made a mistake about my disappearance, I'd been with my grandmother after all. A young policeman, stupid with his own importance, came to check on me the following day.

'Yes,' I said brightly, staring at his badge. 'I love staying with Grannie.'

Enforcer da Cunta was satisfied with his enquiries, and with himself. And that was that. We never spoke about it again.

I saw her one more time. On the way to school a few weeks later, chaperoned by my tired mother, I saw Mimi's face magnified on a screen in a shop window. The missing baby had been found, dead, in a derelict house. There were other children in the basement, corpses rotten with different degrees of decay. The fat man had gone, disappeared without a trace.

The case of the murdered Chinese baby helped the Purists. Their cause was strengthened and not long after the city was divided. My parents were pleased.

They treated me the same way as before, secure that my secret would never be spoken aloud. No one need know I'd been wasted.

But already the baby had started to grow inside me.

Baby

On the outside I looked the same. In my school uniform, I was still Lily White, the slenderest girl in my class.

Concealment was easy at home. My mother averted her gaze if she came upon me undressing for bed. My father didn't come into my bedroom to kiss me goodnight, not after I'd been soiled by the fat man's naked kiss. Bathroom doors were always locked.

Lying in darkness, afraid of sleep, I felt Mimi moving inside me. In my stomach was where she hid, to stop the fat man hurting her.

Sometimes she was angry, trying to get out. Beating me from the other side, groaning. Desperate. Baffled by the fury of pain forced on her small body.

Other nights she was quiet and sad. But I knew she was still there.

One night I woke screaming, 'I'm sorry. I'm sorry, Mimi.'

My mother stood watching me in the dark. I know

she heard me. She replaced my cover and left the room without speaking.

When my skirt got tight she bought me a new one. 'You're growing up, Lily,' she said. 'Almost 14.'

They couldn't wait for me to grow up and leave home. Get a job somewhere, maybe visit sometimes on a Sunday to keep our relationship respectable.

Mimi was almost fully grown before they noticed her. She couldn't hide inside me much longer. I hid both of us in the closet, scrunched up behind the coats.

They must have hoped I'd gone again, back to the fat man's house, for good this time. But no. I was still there. My father found me as his hand reached to the back of the closet in search of dusty golf clubs.

They took me to the Hospital of Hope. But the doctors were frightened. The rigid new laws recently imposed in Pure World meant they couldn't risk killing a child.

My father signed the forms releasing me and the eight month foetus to the protection of the Sisters of Mercy. As a member of the Pure Party, that must have been hard for him. He didn't believe in God, only law and order. God is much too chaotic.

I adored the Sisters of Mercy, their calm smiling faces behind white wimples. The rituals of prayer and meditation that could release me from the obsessive agony of thoughts about Mimi. The convent was where I mastered controlling my mind.

The baby was born and they taught me how to

care for her. They found me a job in a bakery. This mindless work suited me and I had permission to take the baby with me.

'Put the baby in the garden, by the back door where you can hear her if she cries,' the baker said kindly. But no, I couldn't do that.

She was a good baby but the kitchen was too hot for her. She often cried. We had to leave. But I found another job, arranging flowers for a rich lady who sometimes gave me bags of unwanted food.

I can't say I was happy but nor was I unhappy. My heart was choked and impervious to any more pain.

For years this was my fantasy. The fat man, whose name is Fredo Trap, according to media reports exposing the House of Horror, suggests that I help him steal the baby, the one he has watched play in the dirt alone behind her parents' restaurant.

He asks me and I say, 'No.' Firm, absolute. No need to even ask again. That's a game I will always refuse to play.

Somehow, I am cleverer than him. Braver, stronger. I manage to say no to his perverted game and escape anyway.

What if I had said no? Would fat Fredo have asphyxiated me?

Asphyxiation. It's a gorgeous word. I looked it up in the dictionary at the library. Fredo Trap asphyxiated some of the children. Some of the others were reduced to piles of bones under the floor of the cellar he locked me in for three nights. Too late for an autopsy to reveal the secrets of their end.

Was I lucky to escape? Or is it best to be murdered? I have never successfully answered that question. I change my mind too much. Is Purgatory a worse place than Hell? I do not know.

I could have said no to his game. But I did not say no. I agreed to play. I helped the stinky fat man murder the baby. I was his assistant. His partner in perfidy. His pimp. The baby died a horrible death. I heard it. And she was happy, so happy, only a few minutes before.

But I had no courage left. Three days in his cellar had used up my reserves of courage. I would have done anything to escape.

Maybe you will say it doesn't matter, you were a child yourself, a slight girl of 13. There is no shame in fleeing from evil, running all the way home in the dark, panting, arriving on your parents' doorstep, school regulation white underwear missing. You could say I wasn't to blame.

In hindsight we do everything right. When I took Mimi's hand in mine I should have screamed Run! and dragged her away from the car; not helped her into it.

Maybe you can forgive me for that mistake, even though it was a big one. Maybe I paid for the first Mimi with my own innocence. But not my next betrayal, that one is not possible to forgive.

When I escaped from the House of Horror I made up my mind that I would never make a mistake again. I would never trust anyone or betray anyone. Before long I had broken both those rules.

I abandoned my own baby without a backward glance and punished myself by falling in love with you. I almost convinced myself that I didn't love you, I was using you for diamonds and safety. But I do. Rich, I have always loved you. And with love comes fear.

You should never have taken me to that flesh party. Why did you do that? You are not a bad man. Why did you test me with that? The smell of their bodies as they came close to me. As their sex tools stabbed my sacred part, one after the other, I could smell him. The fat man was lying on top of me, smothering my soul in pursuit of his own pleasure. Why did you take me there?

It doesn't matter now, it's too late for anything but her to matter.

For years I didn't think about her at all. I couldn't think about her. That was my bargain with sanity.

When I realised I had fallen in love with you I was frightened. You adored me. Thought I was perfect. What if you found out about me? I couldn't bear to lose your regard, have you look at me with pity and disgust.

I wanted to tell you. I tried to invent a good story, something you could swallow that would allow me to have the child and keep you.

But as the years passed, it became more difficult.

Why, you would ask, didn't you tell me before? You would wonder how any mother could have left her baby in the House of Abandon all that time, saying nothing.

How had I managed to leave her there in the first place? It sounds impossible now.

She was almost the same age as Mimi when I left her alone on the steps. This baby was also called Mimi. When the nuns had asked for a name, I couldn't think of another. But I always called her Baby.

That worked at first, when she was small. As she grew up, she started to point at herself saying Me Me. She always looked peaceful in sleep. Somehow her serenity hurt me. The love and trust with which she smiled at me.

As she approached her second birthday, I couldn't bear the resemblance to the other Mimi, the one I had murdered. Because I did have a choice. I chose to go into Fredo Trap's shiny black car. Mimi did not choose. I lured her.

Suddenly I couldn't bear to look at my baby girl. I left her alone, locked in the room we lived in, and sat by myself in the library reading about perverts.

Beauty protects children from their advances. That's what the psychologists say. Stand out too much and be free from their naked gaze. They will not come too close to the dazzling light surrounding a beautiful child.

So what was I? The exception to the rule? The child who issued an invitation, who couldn't resist wasting myself? Could that be it?

Yes. I am evil. Evil enough to leave my baby alone all day. She smiled at me when I came home, delighted to see me. No cries of complaint from her, just laughter and extended arms.

I knew I had to get rid of her. It was either that or go mad. It was her or me. I chose me. She waved at me as I walked away, never suspecting it was goodbye.

How could I tell you that?

How could I risk losing you? You were everything that I had, the only good thing in my life. So I kept thoughts of her hidden in my heart, sending gifts to the orphanage for all the children on their birthdays, so that I could secretly celebrate hers.

You noticed my silences, called me mysterious. Made jokes about a secret boyfriend. But you were mine and I was yours. We didn't need anyone else. I believed that, until you betrayed me.

I was a fool for trusting you, for loving you. For breaking my golden rule. But that was my punishment for abandoning my baby, my angel. The first Mimi, that could be blamed on innocence, but I damned my soul with the second betrayal. Premeditated evil always has to be paid for.

And you made me pay, Rich. Was it fun? Was it worth it?

Suddenly I couldn't stop thinking about my lost girl.

I couldn't eat, couldn't sleep. It was almost her 13th birthday. I became obsessed with the idea of saving her. From what? Really I was trying to save myself, to rewrite my past. My life became a nightmare when I was 13.

I made up my mind to tell you. You'd been distant, strange. I think you really did imagine I was in love with someone else.

Slavia prepared your favourite food. I lit lime-scented candles, the bubble smelled fresh and new. As you swallowed oysters, enjoying the choke in your throat, I sat sipping water; screwing up my courage.

I had a mad plan to suggest we adopt a child, a little girl, then later, once we were both used to her, to tell you she was mine.

But casually, without looking at me, you said, 'I thought we might go to a flesh party, for a laugh.' You looked at me. 'We don't have to…might be fun, that's all.'

What did you want from me then? To scream, no, I won't do that? To reveal my roots as a daughter of Purists? To confirm the exclusivity of our love by refusing?

Aware that I was making a mistake, I said, 'Fine, whatever you want.' And carried on not eating my dinner.

Flesh Party

You held my hand on the way in.

Our host greeted us as if it were a cocktail party. The entire gathering filled me with disgust. A crowd of rich, safe fools pretending to be risky.

What are they risking? Sex leads to early death for the flesh girls and leper boys on the other side of the black hole, not this overfed crowd who have all had a double dose of *Safe*. Breaking Pure World's law while the Chief Superintendent of the Dirty Patrol also enjoys the party is hardly living on the edge.

'Isn't transgressing fun?' a big woman asked.

Joining in this cliché is not my idea of fun. Or yours, judging by the look on your severe face. I smiled for both of us, accepting a glass of pussy juice; also known as a Bellini. I detached your fingers and escaped into the crowd.

Soon there was a queue of ancients, richer even than you maybe, and a woman with thick tan legs waiting to fuck me.

But you don't need to be told this. You were

watching. I knew you were watching even though I could not see you.

You want to know what I was thinking as they fucked me? You know that already too. I sent my thoughts to you.

You think it's easy, lying here, pretending, playing the part of perfect whore so soon after the role of wife? You think I don't want to spit on you, disappear from your sight forever?

Eyes always following me, watching me, imagining me. Beauty can be worn out with too much attention, but I have long since abandoned vanity. The camera of your eyes holds no more fear for me. I'd be glad if you found a physical flaw. Some mark to confirm the impurity in me you have always suspected.

And I know now that I love you, really love you. I dreaded giving myself away. Wasting my self. My self is you. Wasting our love. Throwing it away. I almost said it out loud tonight.

No. You cannot make me scream. I lie still, a living corpse waiting for the next violation, remembering the first time, the smell. This is my punishment, my justice, revenge on myself for what I did. The smell. The smell will never stop.

They orgasmed quickly.

The fat man had taken a long time. I dreaded his smell on the bodies in the queue awaiting the pleasures of my flesh. These men smelled of old brandy and expensive cologne; their flesh free from animal odour. Still they smelled of him.

Fredo Trap's scent invaded the room. I had brought it with me. I take it everywhere.

One of them, a youngish man who went limp soon after entering me but kept up the pretence, smelled of baby vomit. He smiled at me after his turn, grateful to me for not exposing his failed performance. I wondered about his baby. And his wife. Was she watching us? Maybe in the torture garden having the time of her life?

More than one of the men who impaled me that night was heavy. The feel of the flabby flesh, the suffocating weight, the pants of pleasure that lack dignity. You think it is easy to suffer that? To pretend it does not hurt me.

Yes, it is easy. No body with its cheap desires can ever damage me like he did.

I would choose the tearing of my own flesh every time over hearing the baby's cries, again, in the dark.

You never asked if I enjoyed the party.

You should not have taken me there, but you did. And now you have to pay the price. We both do.

The next day I went to the House of Abandon. Matron Correction was pleased to see me. Her greedy eyes smiled as she said, 'Your generosity keeps us afloat, Mrs Powers.'

I asked her about the baby, the one left on the steps over ten years ago. 'She must be about 13 now,' I say. 'Almost 13.'

She looked at me with pleasure and pity. 'Most of the babies are left on the steps. We have no idea who they belong to.'

She lowered her eyes, enjoying confirmation of my secret.

I asked to see the children. My eyes scanned the school room in search of Mimi, or whatever they call her now. None of the little girls resembled me.

'There was one child,' Matron Correction said, anticipating a reward if she could find the answer I was looking for. 'We called her Patricia White because of her noble features and alabaster skin. The children shortened it to Trish. Her face could have been on a coin, if she had more of a sense of herself.'

'Where is she?'

'She left us recently. I can make enquiries for you, Mrs Powers. I'm sure we can find her.'

I made my own enquiries.

Every day I looked for her. I even went back to the fat man's house. Mr Fredo Trap had never been traced, but his house was still there opposite the Dirty House. The place they take criminals, even though none exist, anymore, in Pure World.

The space between the building and the road is not that wide. Some passerby may after all have heard me scream.

Why didn't I scream? I had lost my voice. I couldn't scream. I have never screamed since, though many times I have heard Mimi scream. Somewhere where I cannot reach her, too late for me to save her; but I cannot stop trying.

There is a plaque on the big tree overhanging the road. It contains the names of lost children. My name is not on it. I survived. I didn't tell anyone where I had been. My parents did not ask for the address of the fat man's house, though I could have found my way back there blindfold.

A withered bunch of white flowers sits, lonely, at the bottom of the tree. I went to a kiosk and bought armfuls of white lilies to lay in their place. But I didn't have enough heart to return to the tree.

Where is my baby? Across the border in Fleshworld? That's where they go, those lost girls intent on ruin.

I came home full of hate.

My face staring back at me from the wall betrayed nothing. You love that portrait more than me. That used to hurt me. Not now. Not anymore.

I hated you for loving me, making me love you. I wanted you to suffer. I stopped injecting myself. You saw me inject *Safe* on those recordings you watch obsessively? An old show, a rerun, a repeat performance that looks the same because it is. I haven't been inoculated for weeks. Soon the sores will appear, marking my perfect flesh, exhibits of my soiled soul on the surface of my skin.

But nothing happens. My skin stays pure. Maybe I have been soiled so many times, I have developed immunity. Not made of tears or regret, but my bitter pride in survival. My mysterious desire to live in spite of everything.

I could wake up tomorrow morning covered with sex decay sores. I could be infected now, as you watch me undress; while I watch myself reflected in the mirror of your expensive eyes.

I know it is no use searching anymore. I will not find her in Pure World. I have to follow her to Fleshworld.

You don't matter anymore. You stopped mattering when you betrayed our love, made me suffer the smell. Why did you do that? To prove something? To prove you own me? Maybe you do.

I should thank you. You gave me the idea. To sacrifice myself. To swap my life for hers. To go to Fleshworld and take her place. If only it isn't too late.

What will you do? Inside you are lonely like me. I can't help you. You are not helpless, like her. You can find your own solution.

By the time you read this I will be lost in Fleshworld, somewhere you cannot find me. Don't bother to look. I am not Ice anymore. Not your perfect Ice. I'm just another damaged soul who cannot erase her past. I tried to drown my sorrows in the serene green of my bath. But they floated back to the surface to suck me under.

I have to right the wrong I have done. I don't deserve to be safe while she is trapped in Hell. I must find my baby. I have finally made the right choice, choosing her before myself. Choosing her instead of you.

We are the same self. Remember that if you never see me again.

But I did see her again.

I had envied her, resented her silences. And now I understand why sometimes it was impossible for her to speak. Her courage in returning to the fat man's dungeon, that space inside her head, rendered her mute. Ice will never erase the fat man's smell. I will never erase Mother. She is right. We are the same.

Damaged goods.

Is it too late? This time it really is goodbye?

It's best this way. Now she won't find out you fucked me.

I used a test tube.

Your tube.

Shut up.

Motherfucker.

I'm not listening to you.

Ice Queen is dead.

Ice is not dead.

I'd know if she was dead.

I'd feel it.

So where is she?

Did she die in Bad's arms when the House of Abandon exploded?

They went there yesterday. There's no reason why she'd still be there when it blew up. Is there?

Mother's laughter taunts me.

I filled my ears with Ice's favourite music, Mozart's

'Mass in C minor', drowning out the coarse laughter.

It had started to rain while I was reading Ice's story. The fires of Fleshworld are out. My evil creation obliterated. Rain, real rain, falls from the sky cleaning everything it touches with its acid drops.

And she's alive, my Ice, I know she is. I will see her again. My damaged saint. Why couldn't I see her before? Really see her. I was too busy examining myself, magnifying my own faults, to notice her burden.

I've been a selfish, weak fool. And now she's out there in the dark, still suffering. I must find her.

Am I deluding myself? Is it possible to lose my only love and find her again twice? How many miracles can one man claim in a lifetime?

I have been searching for something I had already. By the time I realised, I'd lost it again. Why do I try to control everything when I understand it's impossible?

She will come home. She will find me.

I fell into troubled sleep, exhausted under the weight of this thing stuck inside me which seems to insist that I don't deserve happiness, don't deserve love, don't deserve Ice.

I woke with a sore, open and weeping, on my sex tool before realising I'm still asleep. And that it is not Mother talking. It is me.

Part Three

Utopia

'Anything can happen here, at any moment.'
The Shanghai Gesture

Holding Ice's letter, I drifted in and out of sleep. Her handwriting is so evocative, ink leaking emotion into its curves.

Her voice fills the dark room.

Gone with Bad to the House of Abandon
Never see you again
Abandon with the bad boy
Never see you again see you again

Why did she go to the House of Abandon? Bad knows Trash is not there. He's lying to her. Or Ice is lying to me?

They're in it together.

You're wrong. She loves me. You cannot hurt me anymore.

She needs him.

I can give her everything.

You can't impregnate her.

You saw to that with your scissors.

I woke to the sound of a child crying.

Trash was fast asleep, clutching the locket she never takes off, making no sound except short, faint breaths. I must stop calling her Trash. She has started to smell like Ice. Is she wearing her scent?

I lifted the white sheet, allowing moonlight to reveal her naked form. The chipped paint on her toenails is somehow moving. The number on her foot is hard to make out. But it is still visible.

All the children are stamped and logged, even temporary visitors like me. That is why Ice went to the House of Abandon. To find the number of her child.

Does it matter if Trash is really Ice's child? In my heart I know that she is, I have always known. Somewhere deep in my consciousness, I recognised her in the bar. But I pushed the thought away, along with my other doubts, because I wanted to make use of her.

I will try to make it up to her by looking after her. I must go on trying to save Mimi, that child who no longer exists except in Ice's imagination. By doing that, I may find Ice. Or help her to find her way home to me.

I can still hear the child crying.

I follow the sounds. She is out there somewhere in the night, alone, sobbing.

Downstairs, the sound is louder. It is breaking my heart. Tears never move me. Ice never cries.

Her confession has changed me forever. All the

hurt in me is on the surface, and I cannot bear this child's pain.

I unlock the bubble. And she is there on the iron bridge, sobbing her heart out.

'Baby...Don't cry, you're home.'

She looks very young. I don't even know how old she is. Her tears have washed her face clean of sophistication. That mask of outward serenity, which concealed her heartache, has dissolved. She cannot wear it anymore. She needs to let go.

'Everything is all right.'

She lifts her tear-stained face and says, 'No, Rich, everything isn't all right. Nothing will ever be all right again.'

She has lost heart. For too long she clung to hope, nurturing a happy ending she didn't dare believe in. Now her hope is in ruins, like the devastated city.

'I can't go on,' she sobs. 'I want to die.'

'Take my strength,' I say, putting her hand on my heart.

Over her shoulder, I can see the flesheaters through the trees, closing in on us. I can't help admiring them, despite their repulsive looks. The cold will kill them if they separate and try to fly. So they have changed form, welded on to dead humans to adapt to their new atmosphere.

She allows me to carry her inside and wash her, change her into my big warm pyjamas. She stops crying but will not look at me.

'Baby, you're safe now. I know everything, I read your story. And I love you. I will always love you. I will never let anything bad happen to you again.'

She looks at me coldly. 'Why do you have to own everything? You don't love me. You love Ice. She's a fantasy. An illusion. I am still Lily, that girl locked in the dark, too scared to scream out loud.'

'You came home. You came back to me.'

'I had nowhere else to go.'

'You belong to me.'

'I'm a bad person.'

'Good people sometimes do bad things.'

'I'm bad and it can never be undone. If I'd found her, I'd have had a chance. Only a chance. Not to wipe the past clean, but to invent a future. But I can't go on pretending to be brave.'

Suddenly I am frightened.

What if Ice hates me when she finds out that Trash is her child? I took her baby to Fleshworld. Took her to Hell and left her there. What if Trash tells her she's in love with me? Acts like there's something between us?

Ice imagines her child small and perfect like Mimi, not dirty and damaged like Trash. Trash may not even be Mimi. I could be mistaken. I can't raise my wife's hopes, then fob her off with the wrong girl.

The records have been destroyed in the explosion; secrets of identity lost forever.

Here I am doing it again, concealing what I should be sharing. Am I really protecting Ice from broken dreams? Or is it envy that makes me hesitate: a primal fear she will love the child more than me? But I cannot deny her that choice. Control is not love. True power comes only with freedom.

Any minute she will walk into her own bedroom and find her daughter asleep in her bed. One look at Trash will arouse her suspicions. I saw the way they stared at each other through the walls of the ice cage.

'She's here.'

'What?'

'In your bed. Asleep.'

'The little girl from Fleshworld?'

'Your baby.'

'What?'

'If you hadn't gone to Fleshworld, I'd never have met her. Really she found her own way home.'

Ice looks at me with incomprehension.

'Your child.'

'She's here?'

Ice's hand is trembling, or maybe it is mine shaking. They are clamped tight together, it is impossible to tell.

Trash's white, sleeping face is almost unsoiled of care. She could be any child, safe at home with her parents. Except it's obvious to look at her she could not be my blood child.

There is no outward mark to signal that she has recently escaped from bondage as a flesh girl. I know from Ice's smile that I have done the right thing.

'Look,' she whispers, excited. 'She's still wearing the locket I gave her.'

Lots of girls have fake gold lockets they wear for far too long. I can't spoil Ice's happiness by pointing that out, the joy in her smile.

My wife has lovely teeth. Clean and even and natural. I notice new things about her all the time. Defying my scepticism, she pings open the locket, revealing a picture of herself.

'Me,' she whispers. Closing it carefully, she stares at her baby.

'What happened to her hair?'

'Fire.'

Trash wakes up, rubbing sleep from her eyes.

'Baby,' Ice says.

'Who are you?' Trash asks, sleepy.

'I'm...your guardian angel. Come to kiss you goodnight.'

'You look like an angel.'

'What's your name?'

'Trish...everyone calls me Trash.'

'Everyone is wrong,' her mother says. 'Your name is Angel.'

Pleased with her new name, she falls back into sleep.

We stayed up late, talking, laughing, making plans.

Eventually Ice, exhausted, fell asleep. I watched her serene face, counting her breaths.

I cannot sleep. Fleshworld has been joined once more with Pure World. The black hole swallowed up in the explosion, leaving only a crack where it used to be.

Our city is now called Chaos. There's talk of reinstating its old name London, and the old-fashioned rules of that once respected city.

But it is only a matter of time before the flesh-eaters take control. Only a matter of time before that nightmare without end begins.

The old Rich would have seen an opportunity, invented a poison to wipe out the flesheaters, perhaps even had ambitions to reinvent Luck as the controller of Chaos. Now my plans are focused on transporting us to safety. The rest can be left behind without regret.

I could outrun the flesheaters. Ice and Trash might not make it.

Go on, Rich. Save yourself. Run...

The flesheaters are gathering on the other side of the lake, their metamorphosis almost complete, almost human. I need to destroy the iron bridge; make the bubble impregnable. For now.

They can no longer fly, but it is only a matter of time before they learn to swim. Before they can cross the lake and invade the bubble. Before they eat us alive. Escape is the only safety now.

But how will we get away?

Maybe I do have one last use for Luck. Luck has a flypod. I know where he keeps it. Luck can escape.

You'd have to go alone.

I'd never abandon Ice.

There's isn't enough air in the flypod.

There's enough for two.

She won't leave Trash.

No sense all three of us being eaten?

Leave Trash behind for the flesheaters.

The girl's DNA could be tested. Ice wouldn't leave her daughter behind. But, if it comes to it, would she sacrifice herself for a stranger?

Next morning we had breakfast together, almost a normal family eating pancakes.

Trash does not look like Trash anymore. Ice has dressed her in a pink shirt and a pair of blue jeans. She looks more like Angel.

Trash must be tested for infection. It is tempting to do this without my wife's knowledge. But further secrecy between us is to be resisted.

The old Rich would have taken a sample, conducted a secret test. But that type of secret is really a lie. The choice isn't mine. I must stop trying to control everything. I promised her that.

Ice held the child's hand while I pushed in the needle, emptying *Safe* into her arm. I vaccinated her three times before extracting blood.

We reassured her the result would change nothing. We have to know the truth in order to protect her. We will never abandon her. I don't think she believed me.

She tested negative. Her blood is still pure. When

she saw her mother's brow smooth with relief, the child sank back, breathing out at last.

'It's ok? I'm not…wasted?'

'You're perfect,' Ice replied. 'A miracle.'

I suspect we no longer need *Safe*. But now the flesheaters are in Pure World, no one is safe.

Trash watches them trying to cross the lake, trying to walk on water. As fast as one drowns, another takes its place.

'It's all right. You are safe,' Ice reassures her child.

'But can't they fly?'

'They are too heavy to fly now they have changed form. They would need to separate - metamorphise back into insects - then they would be easy to squash.'

Angel laughs at my explanation, but isn't completely convinced.

'Wouldn't it be fun if we all had new names?' Ice asks, changing the subject.

'You have a name,' Angel says firmly. 'Mummy.'

Ice blushes, looking pleased anyway.

'That makes you Daddy.'

'You're both perfect,' Angel says optimistically.

Her attraction to the bright side is contagious. I find my toe tapping to her songs. I even caught myself singing under my breath. Angel sings all the time and follows Ice around the bubble. A little irritating, but my wife is happy. And I would do anything for her.

Sometimes I catch the girl's eyes following Ice, the

way my own do. She looks anxious, fearing she will never see her again when she leaves the room. Just as suddenly the child becomes excited about something ridiculous like an almond.

'What's that?' she asked, following me down to the storage zone under the bubble to pack supplies for our journey.

I thought she meant the gallons of *Sleep* stored in canisters. *Sleep* was less popular after *Safe* made it possible to breathe again. But she wasn't curious about the big cans of narcotic. The stuff I intended to use on her. She had never seen an almond before. And suddenly she's laughing again, eating too many almonds as I tried to pack them in sterile bags.

I find myself questioning her happiness. Is it the game of pleasing ingrained in her?

No. She smiles in her sleep. She no longer wakes screaming every night. She has not told us what happened in Fleshworld, but we can guess the content of her nightmares. She will tell her mother in time.

Though not everyone finds confession cathartic. Maybe forgetfulness is the best gift a parent can bestow on a child. Sleeping forever better than living in Hell...

There must be another way?

The flesheaters are watching us through the glass walls of the bubble; desiring us. Every day they manage to float a bit closer before drowning in the lake.

'So,' I say to my wife and daughter. 'It's almost time. Where would you like to go?'

'I've heard Utopia's nice,' Ice suggests, joining in the game. She knows already that is where we are going.

'Oh yes,' Angel agrees, 'there's a song about that. An old song they used to play in Paradise...'

Angel stops. Unsettled that she has almost mentioned Paradise Alley, where she was employed as Bad's flesh girl.

'Old songs are the best,' I say, filling the silence.

'You would say that, because you are old,' Ice laughs affectionately.

'But...' Angel looks anxious. 'How will we get out?'

'We'll fly.'

'I can't fly!' Angel says, alarmed.

'We have a flypod,' Ice reassures her. 'It's safe.'

'But how will we get past them?'

'Rich...Daddy will take care of everything.'

She seems sure.

Daddy will put you to sleep forever.

Tomorrow we are leaving.

Tomorrow, everything will be different. For Ice, for Angel, for me. A new start in a world that promises to be cleaner than this one. The future is before us and all we hope for is a blank screen, a clear space to leave our mark. The possibility, at least, of happiness.

Fleshworld is gone. Luck is gone. Mother's voice may never be muted but she cannot hurt me anymore.

The pure scent of Utopia will destroy the fat man's stink, but Ice will never forgive me if I swap Angel's life for hers again.

I make a promise to myself, one that will never be broken. I'm done with evil. Evil breaks Ice. There must be a way to save all three of us.

The oxygen masks were Ice's idea. Insurance if we run out of air. So obvious. Why didn't I think of it? Was I seeking an excuse to leave Trash behind?

I filled the lake with my entire stock of *Sleep* and waited for the flesheaters to drink. There should be time to get the flypod, land on the water, and get my family safely on board before the flesheaters wake up.

I need to have time. I'm gambling our lives on it.

In the morning, with the lake a natural green, more beautiful that it has ever been before, Ice and Angel are waiting as I approach in the flypod.

But when I land on the water, the flesheaters start to wake up. Smelling fear, they try to swim. One of them doesn't drown. It enters the water backwards and manages to flap within a foot of the deck before getting stuck. Ice can't persuade Angel to leave the bubble and get into the flypod.

I open the roof of the bubble, but can't land the pod inside without risking damage. It has to fly us all the way to Utopia.

Ice tells Angel to shut her eyes. She takes the child's

hand and coaxes her onto the deck. Anxiety shows in the almost invisible frown between my wife's eyebrows as she guides her daughter, step by step, into the flypod; allowing us to escape.

Trash's Diary

Angel is upset. She has left her diary behind.

I listen to Ice comforting her daughter while, out of habit, I watch our old home as we fly away from it.

I told myself it was boredom, those lonely days alone, that made me watch her. There are cameras in every room, even the bathrooms. She was never out of my sight. My eyes kept her safe. But I can see that my voyeurism was an unhealthy obsession, a substitute life that was bad for both of us.

The bubble looks sinister now it is devoid of our presence, surrounded by flesheaters struggling to invade. I am about to switch off the screen. We are almost out of range. Soon that world will be behind us forever. And then I see the boy, Bad, rifling around Angel's bedroom.

He knows he has missed us. We are gone for good. What is he looking for?

He picks up her diary. Opens it. Flicking through its pages; he stops to read.

I hesitate. I can magnify the words, snoop into her secrets. Or I can switch off the screen. Curiosity is an enemy and a friend, it is a question of interpretation. If I had known Ice's story sooner, I could have helped her.

This is my last chance. My nose leads me into temptation.

This is the diary of Angel Powers, formerly Trash White

My mother told me if you write something bad, something that happened to you, then show it to someone who loves you, then all the pain goes away. I love her. That is why I can never ever show her this.

Bad told me you can dream as hard as you like, that don't affect the outcome. But I know it does. He is wrong and I am right. Even if just about this one thing. Dreams come true. I want her to love me more than I want him.

When I saw her on the wall here I wanted her to be my mother. I wished and wished really hard. That's why I stole her picture and put it in my locket. I didn't mean to take it. Because he was sad she was lost. And taking something was wrong. He wanted everything about her to stay with him. I could see in his eyes when I wore her dress how sad he was. But I had to take the picture. I knew if I cut it up small enough to go in my locket and kept it close to my heart she'd come back to me.

I knew she was my mother when I first saw her. Is it because she is or because

I want her to be?

I knew her even before that. Bad got wind of a rich lady searching the House of Abandon for her lost baby. He had a plot to change the number on my foot and make me the baby.

But I don't have a number anymore. That flower tattoo was the first thing I did after escaping from Abandon. I love that lily. It was worth pleasuring Bad for it, the first and last time he paid me.

When he found out I'd covered up my identity number, he was real mad. He shook me and shook me and kept asking what I remember about before I was in Abandon. I don't remember nothing. I remember a beautiful lady waving to me on the steps. Was it her? It had to be her. Or is that just something he told me?

He told me lots of stuff about her. Things he'd heard from Matron Correction, who was anxious to help the rich lady. She'd stop at nothing to get what she wants, Bad said. Bad told me what to remember, things about when I was a baby. He told me over and over that I'm that lost girl. He told me I'm 13. I don't remember. I could be 13.

I'm worried. What if she finds out I

stole the picture? Will she abandon me? Leave me somewhere all alone with no way home this time?

She will hate me because I'm not the other girl, her real baby.

Maybe I am her baby? I could be. We almost look the same. She says that. And she would know. She's clever.

But what if she starts to think I'm not her baby? Sometimes I think maybe she doesn't mind if I am or not. Maybe she loves me anyway? But maybe not. Maybe she'd start her search all over again to find her real baby and forget me.

I can never tell her. I can never risk spoiling this miracle. This dream come true, finding her and being with her every day. That would be stupid and she says I'm not stupid, I just haven't had much school. And we can fix that. Together. She can teach me. She can show me everything.

When I grow up I want to be her. I want that more than anything.

She is good. So good she doesn't even know. More than anything I don't want her ever to know my secret in case she doesn't love me.

When he took the blood out of me I was real scared. Is there a test? One that tells your real parents? Kids at

Abandon used to talk about it.

But it's ok. My blood isn't bad. She promised me. She would never lie to me.

'What's wrong?' she asked when she found me sitting quietly looking at the flower on my foot.

Nothing.

'You can tell me. If there is something.'

I know.

'No matter what it is.'

A tear appeared on my cheek. I could feel it.

'It will be our secret. I won't tell anyone else.'

She means him. Rich. I go sick inside when I remember being here with him before. Me liking him isn't criminal. He isn't my real dad. But it's wrong. Because he loves her.

Sometimes I catch him looking at me. It's best we forget all about that, he seems to be saying. Maybe he'd like it better if I disappeared?

Sometimes I think he knows. Rich. Sometimes I think he knows I took that picture I cut up to go in my locket. He doesn't want to spoil it for her. He... sometimes seems to like me?

He's nice to me because she is. Maybe he likes me as well? He came back for me, didn't he? But I got him out of that cage. I didn't tell him what Candy Dark made me do for the key.

But I don't know about Rich. I know I can trust my mother. Know in my heart where you're supposed to know. I belong to her.

I want to be good for her. My mother. All my life I've pretended so's people will like me. Or not be mean to me. But she is worth trying my hardest for. It's not an act, it's real. I'm not pretending anymore. I'm Angel not Trash. Trash is dead.

When she said I could say anything to her, she was letting me know that she would pick me over him. If it comes to it. Would she really? I've never been first before.

I'd never make her choose. He might if he knew about me. I was sure he'd notice the picture was missing. But he had other things on his mind. He never noticed nothing. I thought he'd found out when he slapped me hard in the face. But he never mentioned the picture.

He might want to get rid of me. I don't know for sure. Can you ever really know anything ever? I used to think I didn't understand because I'm stupid. But now I think no one understands.

Last night I dreamed I was in Flesh-world again. I sold my soul to Candy Dark who helped me escape.

Tomorrow we are flying to safety, away from the flesheaters, and Bad and Candy Dark, and all the stuff that might get us. Maybe once we get away from here I can stop worrying that she will find out, maybe the fear will go away when we get to…

Bad stops reading. He has found what he was looking for. He closes the book, staring up at the camera. Looking me in the eye.

Is he planning to follow us?

It doesn't matter. Angel is safe now. He can't spoil that. I will never let that happen.

She will learn to trust me, in time. For Ice's sake, I want that more than anything. For myself too, and the better man I hope to become.

A message appears on my screen. Flashes up then disappears.

Your secret is safe.

Bad slips the diary inside the pocket of my jacket, the one he's wearing; saving the rest for later. More dirty details to blackmail me with, I almost feel sorry for the boy. He's in my shoes now. In my house, watching the film of me fucking my wife.

At least I have a chance for salvation. Something in me longed to escape the control of money and power even before I fell in love with Ice. Bad has nothing but his greed. He is me without the sex scar. Me without Ice's love. He has nothing holding him back.

He looks up at the spy camera and winks; then magnifies the flesh flick. It isn't me in the film; it's Bad.

A figure looms behind him, the shadow visible but the form out of shot. The shape is familiar. Is it Mother? She's watching him now. He's the bad one.

It cannot be Mother. She is no longer with us. Luck was destroyed in the flames of Fleshworld, returning me to myself.

So who is that hovering behind Bad? Are the flesheaters in the bubble already?

Ice comes into the cockpit in time to catch a glimpse of Bad before our old home disappears from view. She turns away from the screen, towards me. Did she notice the sex tape?

'Goodbye home sweet home,' Ice laughs, absently touching her stomach. She smiles at me. I smile back, the insecure smile only she sees. Home for me is where she is.

'You know that boy isn't bad looking. Reminds me of you.'

'You met him before?'

'Yes. When I was looking for Angel. He said he had just the girl for me. But I was finished with false promises. I knew she was in Fleshworld. That was my nightmare.'

'And then I took her there.'

She touches my hand, saying nothing. I love her touch, crave it, become lonely for it sometimes even when she's in the room.

Everyone else disappears when she is near. I can feel her presence, without turning my head. In silence she can still be heard.

We stare at the clouds, white and lost. The horizon is full of pictures. The longer you look, the less you see, until eventually nothing is visible. I know she has forgiven me. I know she loves me. But can I forgive myself?

'Do you think she looks like me?'

'She almost looks like you,' I answer truthfully.

Ice looks down into the clouds, feeling their flimsy power. Dreaming is important.

'If we keep flying straight for the mountain we can crash and die happy.'

But we will not crash, not today.

'Why don't you wake her?'

And my wife and daughter are with me for our first glimpse of the island. There it is, up ahead. Now you see it, now it disappears. Look, there it is again.

Angel is overcome with excitement, the lost diary forgotten. She has brought back to life a part of me I feared was dead forever. The trust Mother took from me has returned. I can love without anticipating punishment. Believe at least in the possibility of happy endings.

Despite everything, Ice never lost that ability to love. She thought she did. But her longing to save her baby, to rewrite the false end that killed her own childhood, kept her heart alive.

And the best gift we can give to this child who never lost faith in dreams, whose hope never died under the weight of evidence of evil, is a new set of memories to heal her old fears.

'Is that it?' she asks, face sparkling with joy. 'Is that Utopia? I never knew a place like that could exist. It's like a dream.'

'It is a dream,' Ice tells her. 'A new dream for us.'

I can feel my phone vibrating. One last message, before I am out of reach.

It is from me. A reminder set and forgotten? Something written in the past which can only be understood in the future. What do I have to say to myself?

I could delete it without looking. But I have to look. I never could resist knowing.

This is not the end.

The message is from Bad. He is me now.

He can distribute my new product *Happy*. I considered calling it *Lucky*. But Luck is best forgotten.

Will *Happy* sell better than *Safe*? *Safe* was an instant best-seller, fuelled by fear.

Finally, I understand. It is not desirable to stay safe forever. To stay safe, you can't come too close. Being close to Ice heals me and makes me vulnerable.

Identity is not fixed. That is something I have learned on this strange journey. The mark of evil can be erased. The past stays the same, but I can change.

Stains on the soul are not indelible, they can be loved clean.

A new message flashing, unread, on the screen.

See you soon.

The End

By the same author:

Lampshades
Dead Glamorous
Penniless in Park Lane
Spying on Strange Men

Coming next from Carole Morin:

Liberace's Love Child

'When I was seven, my mother hired me to murder my father. I'd always wanted to be an assassin. It all seemed so easy.
Then it all went wrong...'

www.carolemorin.co.uk

龙
Dragon Ink
London